The Blinks
'Worry'

By Andrea Chatten

Illustrations by Rachel Pesterfield

First published in 2015 by
The Solopreneur Publishing Company Ltd
Cedars Business Centre, Barnsley Road, Hemsworth,
West Yorkshire WF9 4PU

www.thesolopreneur.co.uk

ISBN 978-0-9931880-7-7

Printed in the U.K.

For further copies please go to - www.oodlebooks.com.

Also available on Amazon and Kindle.

Dedication

This book is dedicated to Lily, Alfie &
Estelle, and to all the children who I have
had the pleasure of working with over the
years, you know who you are!

It is also for my wonderful Mum, and my
very much missed Dad who is a morsel of
goodness in one very special Blink.

CONTENTS

Chapter 1

Amanda

Let me introduce you to Amanda.

Amanda is 9 years old and lives with her mum, dad and younger brother Tom, in a normal house on a normal street on the edge of a normal Northern City called

Sheffoold. If we compare Amanda to other children, we would say that she has a pretty good life, is well loved and should be perfectly happy in her childhood. The problem with Amanda is that she has always been a bit of a worrier and slowly, over time, her worrying has made her feel anything but normal.

Can you remember your first memory? Was it riding a bike? Falling from a swing? The arrival of a younger brother or sister? Well, Amanda's first memory at the tender age of 3 was, in fact, a worry. What do you think 3-year-olds might worry about? Losing her favourite toy? Whether or not she might get the chance to paint when at pre-school? No!

Amanda's first memory and perhaps her first ever worry was that Brenda, the lovely old lady who lived across the road, would one day not be able to get up her front door steps! This worry bothered Amanda for months, and she was only reminded of it yesterday when, as she walked home from school, she saw Brenda sweeping up the front path.

Amanda carefully crossed the road. "Hi Brenda, how are you today?"

"Hello Amanda, well just look at you, haven't you grown?" Brenda replied in a gentle, quavering voice; the sort that older people seem to have.

Amanda blushed, but secretly she loved that Brenda had said this.

Over the last few months, Amanda had been worrying that her brother Tom was already nearly as tall as her, and he was two years younger!

"I'm going to see if I can bake a cake this weekend Brenda, would you like me to bring you a piece?" Amanda beamed.

One feeling that she did like was the one that came with doing kind things.

"Ooh, yes please. That will make my afternoon cup of tea feel like a real treat. I do like your cakes, Amanda." And then

Brenda did something that took Amanda quite by surprise. She did a little jump in the air with a sideways kick.

Amanda couldn't believe that Brenda, who must be at least 120 (actually she's a spring chicken at 80), had done something so energetic after clearing the path, and knowing that she still had the steps to do.

Brenda and Amanda said their goodbyes and Amanda hurried home, her mind now bombarded with troublesome thoughts. What if they didn't have any flour? What if Mum said she couldn't bake a cake? What if Brenda tried to do such crazy moves while on one of the steps?????

So as you can see Amanda's little worries had become stronger and stronger as time went on. Her brain seemed to be very good at it, as she now worried about EVERYTHING.

In fact, Amanda was so good at worrying that if it were made into an Olympic sport Amanda would get a gold medal no problem. Actually, the Olympic Board would be so impressed with her talent that they would issue a one-off, super rare, triple platinum medal just for Amanda!

Here is a list of some of the things that Amanda worries about:

1. Brenda's steps.
2. Brenda jumping on her steps.
3. Getting up in the morning.
4. Getting to sleep.
5. Tom having bigger feet than her.
6. Tom growing faster than her.
7. Growing up.
8. Not being clever enough.
9. Not being pretty enough.
10. Forgetting do her homework.
11. What to wear.
12. What not to wear.
13. Maggie & the Meanies.
14. What if her friends didn't like her new coat.
15. People who like her.
16. People who might not like her.
17. What they were having for tea

tomorrow.

18. What if the hamster died.
19. Robbie being a boy and them being good friends.
20. What if she ended up being an actress and forgot her lines when she was performing in front of the Queen!

And this is only page 1 of 2,821,910!

Amanda was a good-hearted girl, who had been brought up to be a kind friend and respectful to people. She always tried her best in class too and although she wasn't the cleverest, she wasn't the dumbest either. Her well-brushed, long hair, clear eyes and funky freckles, meant she was pretty cool; more so when she smiled and laughed.

Sadly this was happening less and less due to the worrying, and Amanda saw none of the good things that other people saw in her.

Amanda's worrying was even starting to spoil her friendships. The person that all her friends loved being with was slowly disappearing. Amanda no longer wanted to run around the playground playing Tig.

Gone were the days when she had made all her friends laugh with silly songs, and then all of them doing funny dances to them. Most days Amanda felt like her worrying was eating away her life.

Amanda used to have loads of friends. She and Robbie would happily flit from one group of friends to another. This didn't happen so much anymore. Partly because she was now worrying that people might think that Robbie was her boyfriend! Even though they had been best friends since nursery, and everyone knew that.

But mostly, Amanda worried that people might not want to play with her because she just wasn't as much fun anymore. She had noticed that other children in her year group always seemed to be in the middle of something if ever she and Robbie tried to join in.

This is what confirmed to Amanda that Robbie was her all-time best friend. Robbie had never fallen out with her or decided he did not want to be friends anymore. Robbie just liked Amanda for who she was.

One playtime Amanda and Robbie were first out for a break and looked at the empty playground. "What do want to do today, Amanda? Oh, have I showed you my latest diablo trick? It's awesome." Robbie squealed excitedly and began spinning and grinding the hourglass shaped piece of green plastic onto the black wooden poles and string.

Every day, Amanda was reminded that Robbie was the absolute best friend she could ever have. He made her laugh, he never got cross with her (even though he could sometimes get cross quickly at other things), but most of all Amanda felt that she liked herself the most when she was with Robbie.

Luckily Robbie felt exactly the same way and as friendships go this was probably the most equal and caring friendship you could get. Nevertheless, Robbie had noticed a change in Amanda over the last few months and now felt a good time to talk to her about it.

"You don't seem happy anymore, Amanda. Has something happened?" asked Robbie.

Amanda didn't know what to say so mumbled, "No I'm absolutely, totally and utterly fine." This was such an obvious lie, and if the words didn't give that away then the way she said it certainly did. Amanda then instantly started worrying about the fact that she'd just told a little fib to her best friend.

"You are still my best friend, aren't you?" Robbie asked, in a way that couldn't hide his hurt.

"Of course I am," Amanda whispered. She thought she saw a tiny tear in the corner of her friend's eye. This worry could stop Amanda from sleeping for a week!

"Do you ever worry about stuff, Robbie?" Amanda asked bravely. She was almost scared of the answer.

After several minutes of diablo throwing and amazing catching, Robbie replied, "Of course I worry. Doesn't everyone? I once worried that my little brother was going to tell everyone that I fancied Kiera Moward, because that would have been a nightmare. He opened my spy journal and saw, written there in gold gel pen, – Robbie fancies Kiera".

"Did he tell anyone?" Amanda asked, already worrying at the thought of her little brother doing the same thing to her.

"No, thank goodness." Robbie continued, "I really wanted to hurt him, but I knew he would cry and then my mum would want to know what it was all about, and I would get into trouble like I always do. So instead, I told him that if he ever told anyone about Kiera, then I would tell everyone he does the smelliest trumps!"

Amanda was just about to say something else when she noticed that the rest of the school were scurrying around them having playtime fun. But she really wanted him to know how she was feeling and so made a promise to herself to talk to him some more later on.

Little did Amanda know though, that she was about to be part of something very special and someone was going to help her in more ways than one.

Chapter 2

The midnight meeting

"Sssshhhhhhhhhh. Order. Order"

Silence quickly fell upon the specially selected room which was filled with energy driven little folk. The respect for their Guide was obvious.

This was the start of the midnightly meeting where all The Blinks (from the town where you live) meet for some very serious business. I say the town where you are because every town all over the world is supported by these wonderful carers of young hearts and souls.

Whichever Continent you are in, anywhere on planet Earth, The Blinks are there somewhere around you. You may never see them as they are too precious and special for everyone to know of them, but you might, from time to time, be lucky enough to meet one or to feel their magic.

And so, there in a local bakery, began the special gathering. This is where all The Blinks of Sheffoold put forward the stories of the unhappy local children to the Executive Blink Panel.

Chief Blinks always choose a bakery as the venue for the nightly meetings because of the warming linger of deliciousness and joy that remains, even at night, after a busy baking day.

There's no doubt that most people feel a sense of niceness when entering a shop filled with the warm scent of freshly baked bread and cakes. Although it's known that some of the sweetness leaves with each customer, a wave of their happiness and warmth stays. It's this combination of positive sensations that provides the perfect environment for The Blinks to get to work.

Chief Blink climbed the platform and greeted her valued workers. "Good evening, soul mates. Thank you all for your efforts today checking the happiness needs of the children and young people or for helping them with their choices during their difficult times. We salute you." A gentle cheer rang out from the crowd, a celebration of good; a warming glow of satisfaction and pride lit up the room.

"Our work for this evening must now begin and we need to discuss the findings of the day," continued Chief Blink. "Blinks you know what to do."

Upon this instruction, The Blinks scattered to various positions in the bakery. Each Blink knew the order well, as each place represented a certain stage in each child's journey to better times.

Each Blink would visit the chosen place in the bakery depending on where he or she was in their project. You will learn more of this process as the tale unravels, but in simple terms the stages are as follows....

Stage 1...On the lookout! This phase involves searching for kids who are not as happy in their life as maybe they could be. Being a child isn't always easy; as I am sure you will agree! And growing up, well we all know how hard that can be too.

Getting things wrong and making mistakes can cause some young people to feel pretty sad from time to time. The Blinks involved at this stage are either still checking things out or are close to selecting a child who they feel needs urgent Blink wisdom.

These Blinks go straight to the empty chocolate éclair trays which sit in the main display cabinet just in front of the till. It's here that The Blinks chat about the children who they have noticed throughout the day. Any Blinks that have had a less eventful day, and are perhaps still waiting for a child in need, get the very important job of creating the sugar dough buffet.

This job involves collecting together all the morsels of sweetened crumbs that have been left over in the tiny corners of the Bakery equipment, after clearing away that day. The scrumptious feast that awaits The Blinks at the end of the get together is a highly deserved way of having fun and celebrating. The Blinks buzz off tiny sugar dough strands and they are very much in need of the energy that it provides for their busy, active lifestyles. Being so kind and helpful requires rich fuel which they burn off quickly.

Stage 2...A good start. This part involves The Blinks who are already working with a child and everything is going well. These Blinks share each other's tales of the day and learn from each other's successful actions. This stage also acts as a top-up stage for the soul of The Blinks.

They love the feeling, as we all do when we are getting it right and things are going well. This stage is needed to fill up their feel good bucket, which is then shared with children during the project.

All of stage 2 occurs on the vanilla slice board which is also placed in the main display cabinet, but is in the furthest corner from the door. This area is very rarely full of Blinks. This might surprise you. The reason that this stage is usually the least busy is because most projects or challenges involve finding solutions to problems.

Only rarely do we have moments of total bliss - that is hopefully the feeling we are rewarded with at the end! So, just like us, The Blinks never find the whole thing easy peasy but are luckily too wise to struggle alone. They know that the best answer is gained by seeking the opinion and help of others.

Stage 3...Help! This is the most popular stage of The Blink cycle and includes all The Blinks who are already paired up with a child and are working together, but need regular help themselves from the wiser ones. This is always the busiest meeting point and happens on the wooden bread shelves that span the whole back wall of the bakery, behind the display counter.

This position could also be known as Blink school!

It's here that the Wise ones teach and pass on the important values and morals that are needed in order to get the best possible result for each young person involved. The Blinks understand how important it is to teach and guide future generations of The Blinks, if their work is to continue.

Stage 4...Eye spy. The Blinks that have recently finished a project, and the young person involved has succeeded in improving the situation, are part of this penultimate stage. This meeting happens on the fairy cake trays which sit in the window of the bakery and are usually hidden under large white sheets of disposable paper, making The Blinks feel like they are camping!

This is also a very lovely part of The Blink cycle, as they are hopeful that the child in question is now okay. However, The Blinks do not fully move on until they are 100% sure that all is right, and so the real loveliness only begins after a time of observation has occurred. Most Blinks like to think of this as a watchful eye for a while, should they need to be on hand to help if things slip backwards. The Blinks also have two rules at this stage too;

a)   Each child must tell someone that they trust about how they have been feeling recently and how they are feeling now. The Blinks see this as a very, very important part of the process for many reasons. Everyone needs to know that they have someone who they can trust whether it be a friend, teacher or family member.

Also, by trusting other people with our problems we ask them to be part of our lives, so that they can look after and care for us when we need it most. This also allows The Blinks to feel that they can move on to the next stage. By knowing that each child is okay and that they have some support, completes the circle of Blink magic.

b)   You must never ever under any circumstances mention The Blinks help. Those who have done in the past, and there have been a few, have undergone many strange looks and conversations with people who were convinced that the child was sickening with some delirious illness! But also, The Blinks' input stops from the very moment that those words are uttered, and Blink magic if looked after, can live long in the hearts of grateful children.

Stage 5...Whey hey! Once The Blinks have the total satisfaction that the child has found their place in happier times, it's then, and only then, that the celebration of goodwill can begin. For seven days after the completion of the project, beginning at midnight of the following day, a period of fun begins.

New clothes, sports activities, yummylicious food and day trips out allows The Blinks to restock each positive value in their hearts. This is essential to continue The Blinks success, especially after donating their hearts to whoever just needed their help.

It has been known at this stage for older wiser Blinks to just sleep. How they manage to do so is magic in itself as the younger Blinks are thriving off the feelings of a job well done and sharing their feelings of euphoria (eu – for –i– a = a feeling of true happiness).

Each and every Blink knows the system inside out and knows their role. Even though they aren't the quickest little folk (too many friends to say hello too!), they always get to the correct place and commit to whichever stage they are in.

The Blinks also know they only have until 3am, when Rosie the Baker arrives

to create the delights ready for the day
ahead.

This may be a suitable time to tell you a
little bit more about The Blinks. You will
never ever meet a generous more caring
soul than that of a Blink. Their philosophy
is simple "If you don't know what to do in
a situation, do the kindest thing". And this
is the rule that they live by because this is
how they were created.

Most of the happiest people of the world
are usually the kind ones; and even at
the point of dying, those who give with
love throughout their lives are still giving
kindness, even at the very end. Whenever
one of the earth's kindly folk is passing
on to whatever is next, they release a last
morsel of goodness to the universe and
it's from these caring acts that The Blinks
have developed.

They are made up of all the love,
kindness and wisdom of every person who

has ever lived. They could have fragments of your Great Great Great Grandparents, your ancestors from way back, or even someone you lost recently. This could be why there's always a feeling of familiarity for those who are lucky enough to have a meeting with a Blink, as maybe your hearts have connected before.

Chapter 3

Evolution

The meeting was well underway by now. The bakery was filled with the delicate buzz of The Blinks chattering away. You see The Blinks had to be careful about getting the need just right. If the need isn't the right need, or The Blinks help the child too early, or maybe do too much of the work, then.... Well, I am sure that you can work out that it wasn't as glorious as when we get things right.

However, all Blinks have made mistakes along the way; as it is from the things that haven't gone so well that The Blinks always learn the most, and this is what has made them so wise.

Nobody really knows how long The Blinks live for, but many of The Blinks gathering in the Bakery that night were as old as old could be. As well as a name, each Blink has a tag number which some believe could represent their number in the evolution of The Blinks' population. So, the smaller the number, the older they are.

Each Blink's creation takes many years to evolve. Each speck of love or wisdom is smaller in size than a breadcrumb. It is, however, a crumb shaped purple fluff ball. These purple fluff balls pepper our Universe until they collide or connect with other fluff balls to make a larger and larger mass.

It takes exactly 419 fluff balls to create one Blink and the 420th is the piece that injects the magic. This surge of power causes The Blink to whizz into action. A super force, known as Blink Gravity, then steers them to the nearest Bakery ready to begin their work.

The Blinks work forever. Because to them, what they do isn't a job, it's a total pleasure. Some Blinks believe they are thousands of years old. They talk of helping children from way back.

One Blink prides himself on a time when he helped a child from caveman times face his fear of woolly mammoths. It is thought that when Rednose was getting to the age ready to hunt, he became frozen with fear at the thought of the huge animal he might need to attack.

This fear made poor old Rednose very sad. He began to feel a failure to his father and all the other cavemen in his tribe, which as you can imagine fuelled the fear even further.

You see fear was a vital feeling at that time in history. So was killing animals in order to survive. It was normal. It needed to be done. Blink 672 - Frank Fear-Not helped Rednose realise that fear was making the mammoth seem bigger.

Once Frank Fear-Not explained the facts, Rednose began to understand and accept this as part of his life. He also worked on breaking down the fear and anxiety which was living in his head. Blink Fear-Not also managed to get the message to Bignose, Rednose's father, that providing him with a man size sharpened spear may help take away some of Rednose's fear.

On Rednose's tenth birthday, Bignose presented him with a wonderful handcrafted tool with a mighty piece of impressive flint that was securely attached with plaited mammoth veins. Rednose had never seen anything so beautiful. The spear made Rednose feel important. It made HIM feel powerful. He was not going to let this tool down. The spear had been the final act in getting rid of the fear.

Rednose felt prepared, and, even though, the mammoth was still huge, it now seemed to look realistic. He could do this; especially with his team of men! Rednose went on to become a recognised hunter in the area. His father also became known as Spearman, rather than Bignose, which did his self-confidence a lot of good too!

The Blinks entertained themselves with many stories at the end of a project and the new Blinks listened and learned. New Blinks were being created all the time and were never made to feel awkward attending their first meeting.

They were seen as a natural part of the midnight meeting, just like the sugar dough buffet. And because every Blink had once been a new Blink they were welcomed with open arms and quickly made to feel like they belonged.

By now the meeting was thriving. As the clock ticked away in the bakery, all sorts of situations were talked about.

Tilly is a perfectionist. Many times she has been known to give up on her guitar practise because she wants to be brilliant at it straight away.

Ralphie is a very sensitive soul. He is easily hurt by thoughtless playground talk.

Georgie is still young and does not always understand the importance of getting over a situation and moving on. I am sure if we were honest this is sometimes a problem we all feel, no matter how old we are.

Each child's situation was valid in their own right and many could have benefited from the little changes that The Blinks could help with. But one case stood out and took all The Blinks attention straight away, Amanda!

Chapter 4

Maggie & the Meanies

Amanda worried herself for days about when she was going to finish the chat with Robbie. Some people may have just made time for it if it were that important, but Amanda wasn't very good at that. You see Amanda was beginning to feel that she was stupid for worrying all the time, and this as you can imagine made it worse.

On more than one occasion, Amanda had actually found herself saying "you are so stupid, Amanda. All you do is worry, and everyone thinks you are stupid too." Although this was only going on in Amanda's head as a thought, she was now beginning to feel it.

The days also seemed so full. Everyone was so busy doing things that it stopped Amanda talking to Robbie on her own. What Amanda didn't realise was that a fellow classmate, Maggie, was taking a lot of interest in Amanda at this time.

Maggie used to be a really beautiful popular girl in class, and she and Amanda had once spent a lot of time together. They were both seated next to each other on the carpet on the very first day they started school. Maggie had once been incredibly kind to Amanda; and, even at that very young age, looked after her when she was showing the first signs of worrying.

Nobody quite knew what went wrong with Maggie, but the change was not only noticeable in her ways but most obvious in her looks. Maggie was losing her beauty and looking meaner and uglier every day. The meaner she got, the uglier she became.

Some people say it all happened when she never won the poetry competition in Y2, others say it was when The Meanies started bullying her. Sadly, poor Maggie made many wrong choices and decided to join them rather than be their target, and very quickly occupied the top slot in their gang.

I suppose you are wondering why The Blinks never became involved and helped Maggie at her difficult time? Well, many Blinks tried. Maggie was stubborn and not mature enough to put in the effort needed. If she didn't want to change, she wouldn't.

The Blinks you see can only help those who want to be helped. Although they are always helpful and kind, they cannot do the magic without us wanting it to happen. Maggie's downfall was that she liked how she had become, she felt powerful.

This is why Maggie started focussing on

Amanda. Although Maggie loved power, she was actually quite weak. She didn't have the power of a pacing tiger, or of a superhero, or even of Steven Powell, the toughest judge on TV talent shows. Maggie had about as much power as a toddler having a tantrum. She could create a big performance but was never going to be able to do anything with it.

Maggie was weak and sad and actually quite lonely. Not that she would ever let herself think that, never mind admit it. That is why Maggie targeted the weak and used The Meanies to strengthen her.

The Meanies were also weak, even weaker than Maggie. There were four of them altogether....

Asif Ahmed - titch! Asif was the smallest boy in the class and always had been, right from the infants. He was sick of it. He hated being small and so his frustrations were always there.

He wished to be bigger every day. Asif had to be noticed somehow, so got it by being a pain! Asif loved it that Maggie had made him second in command. This meant that together Maggie and Asif did most of the planning.

Andrew Munroe - wimp! He was the kind of kid that wasn't at all good at very much, but seemed to have mastered the art of being annoying. In class he always interrupted.

He was the one who the teacher always needed a word with at the end of the lesson, and the one who borrowed your stuff but never gave it back. He was a silent member of the crew and just did what everyone told him to do.

Joanne Hotchkiss – fool! Do you want someone to pour water over the teacher's head? Then Joanne is your girl. Joanne had so little regard for herself that she would do anything that people asked because that made her feel popular.

Little did she realise that she was like a puppet and people used her for their entertainment. She was the class fool and watching her get into trouble afterwards was all part of the show for her classmates. Joanne was also a 'yes' person. This meant that she said yes to anything whether she agreed or not. Maggie valued this quality.

Toyla Woods– sly! Toyla hated school. Every day since the day she started she had been called Toylet by her classmates.

This made her hate everyone, and she always hoped that bad things would happen to all the people who had called her names. Toyla loved being part of The Meanies because she got to act out her revenge.

So Maggie gathered her Meanies around her and told them that she had found their next target. Asif and Maggie were worthy leaders of the crew, and they liked the fact that they were surrounded by Joanne, Shaun and Toyla, who would agree with anything. Without the brains of Maggie and Asif, the others would be nothing.

As Maggie went on to explain the situation, the others listened with interest. Amanda was the perfect victim and everyone agreed. But before the fun could begin some serious planning was needed.

Chapter 5

Worry clouds

Amanda woke having had a terrible night's sleep. Her mind would not switch off from the conversation with Robbie. What if Robbie ever fell out with her? Who would she be with at playtime? How would she make new friends? What if her little brother opened her password journal?

She woke up feeling groggy, in a bad mood and not looking forward to school at all.

Amanda hated those nights. Have you ever had them? Although you are comfortable and warm, there's a part of your mind that you know is not going to let the sleep kick in. The worst thing for Amanda was that the longer she lay awake, the more she worried. Not just little worries. Amanda's worries got bigger and bigger and she felt more and more anxious.

A night like this involved many hours of restless movements. No wonder Amanda was tired in the morning, she had completed a duvet marathon in the time that she was supposed to be sleeping! Amanda did not know how to change these worries, which is why this felt like the perfect case for The Blinks.

Although this was all The Blinks had heard so far, Blink 210504 -Will Worry-Less had presented such a good case that the panel agreed for him to become involved. Will Worry-Less would help Amanda before the impact caused more damage. His mission was to make sure that Amanda did not have any more days or nights like that again.

So, as soon as the meeting ended Will Worry-Less headed out into the night and straight over to Amanda's house.

Step 1 was to help Amanda's mum help Amanda.

Mrs Leaper was a good mum but like many mums she was busy. She knew that Amanda did not seem happy at the moment, but she was not sure what to do to change it. She just hoped that love and time would sort everything out.

Mrs Leaper had also noticed that Amanda was not looking as healthy as she once had, and she was also more prone to coughs and colds. She had, however, talked herself into the fact that this was just normal for Amanda's age and it would all naturally get better.

Will Worry-Less felt differently, but knew that Mrs Leaper caring so much was the best start to any problem being solved. All

45

that was needed were a few helpful tips.

When Will Worry-Less found Mrs Leaper, she was fast asleep, on her back, making an unusual whimpering snore! This was the perfect position for Will Worry-Less to get to work.

Without Mrs Leaper knowing anything about it (and The Blinks usually found this technique to work the best) he reduced himself to the size of a little fingernail and sat in the cosy shelf of her inner ear. From here he began nudging Mrs Leaper's thoughts. He also had a quick dabble with the advice valve which

instantly activated the gut reaction system.

The gut reaction system is a part we all have, but sometimes forget to trust. Have you ever been in a situation where someone is making a suggestion that makes you feel uneasy? Do you get a funny feeling that happens in your lower stomach? That is your gut reaction system.

Sometimes it's the power of the Universe informing you that this situation may be difficult but worth doing, or should be avoided at all costs. But more often than not it's The Blinks helping you to help yourself and trust your thoughts and feelings. Even Rednose needed help in this area in order to know the right or wrong time to attack the woolly mammoth.

After several hours of gentle suggestions and fool-proof techniques, Will Worry-Less left Mrs Leaper. He felt satisfied that Mum would be a wonderful support to Amanda the following day when she was feeling overwhelmed with worries.

Step 2 was to quickly pop into Amanda and suggest, whilst she slept, that she needed to talk to her mum about all of her worries, as keeping them locked tight inside was making the problem bigger. Amanda had nearly told her mum a while ago but felt that the problem sounded stupid, and if her little brother Tom found out then she would never hear the end of it.

Will Worry-Less perched himself on Amanda's left inner ear. He then blew in some self-confidence crystals that would dissolve and trickle into Amanda's mind. These would help Amanda realise that if it were a big problem for her then it was a big problem for the people who cared about her, especially her Mum.

Will Worry-Less then perched himself on the tree outside Amanda's bedroom window and waited for morning to break.

Mrs Leaper awoke as normal the next day, slightly earlier than the children in order to wake them and begin breakfast. As she walked into Amanda's bedroom, her gut reaction yelled from deep in her belly that something was definitely wrong.

"Good morning, Amanda. Time to wake up." Mum spoke gently but loud enough to stir Amanda from her sleep.

"Ooooooh," whimpered Amanda in a weak, drowsy voice.

"Are you okay, Amanda? You don't sound too good," said Mum.

"It feels like I've only just gone to sleep. I hardly slept last night, Mum." Amanda spoke nervously; worried that she might get told off.

"Oh, sweetheart. Has this been going on for a while?" Her mum asked, feeling the strong vibes bellowing from her lower tummy, which directed her to get into Amanda's bed and hold her tightly under the covers.

"Ages, Mum, I lay here most nights with my brain just sending me lots of things to worry about."

A flush of horror spread across Mrs Leaper's cheek. "I'm so sorry Amanda. Why didn't you tell me?"

"Because I felt silly and embarrassed. Do you think I'm silly Mum? Are you cross with me?" This suggested that Amanda was feeling rather small in the arms of her lovely, warm, mum.

"Of course not," Mum replied, stroking Amanda's cheek. "But I do wish you'd told me sooner. Listen, darling, we don't have time to sort this now, but I promise we'll discuss it tonight. Is that alright with you?"

"Thanks, Mum," sighed Amanda, already feeling the relief that she was no longer alone with her problem.

"Right then, let's get ready for school." Mum swished open the curtains and the daylight flooded in sending colour and light around the bedroom like a rainbow. Will Worry-Less looked on from outside the window, feeling content that his night's work and some rainbow magic were already making the day ahead feel better for both Amanda and Mrs Leaper.

Amanda's day did feel better. She didn't have as strong a feeling that all her worries were just hers; somehow knowing that Mum knew made Amanda feel hopeful that things were going to improve.

Mum, however, spent all day with

Amanda at the forefront of her thoughts. Her mind was now racing with possible solutions that may help Amanda stop worrying so much, and more importantly to teach her how to sleep better.

That evening Amanda began her bedtime routine. It was never a 'late to bed night' on a school night. Amanda's mum and dad did let her and Tom stay up a little later on a weekend. They both knew that sleep was an important part of being able to learn well at school, and so Amanda always went to bed at a reasonable time.

Amanda's bedtime routine was the same every night.

7.45pm Pyjama's on (unless it was a shower night which was usually every other night). Supper cuddles and time for reading a book. This took place in Amanda or Tom's bedroom, whose ever turn was next. This time together was spent talking about what had happened that day and

also included lots of reasons why they
were so loved.

8.00pm(ish) Teeth brushed and then
into bed. Each day always ended with love
no matter how difficult the day had been.
Mum and Dad always forgave, once the
lesson had been learned.

8.15/8.30pm Tucked up in bed.
However for Amanda the night ahead was
not going to be fluffy and dreamlike. The
putting to bed job would have usually
been finished now, and Mum would be
wandering downstairs to start some of the
jobs that mums and dads do when their
children are sleeping peacefully in bed.
However, tonight was going to be different.

Amanda was her usual unsettled self,
but she remembered that Mum had
promised that morning that they would
talk later on. So she waited patiently,
desperate for Mum not to have forgotten.
At that moment, Mum popped back into

her room and sat on the bed for a lovely cuddle.

"Come on then, what's the matter, Darling?" Mum asked in a gentle, bedtime sort of way.

"My brain is making me think of all of these silly thoughts, Mum. I just can't switch my stupid brain off."

"Come on, tell me some of these thoughts and we will see which ones are helpful and which ones are unhelpful," Mum replied, quite surprised at herself for feeling so confident about tackling this issue.

"Okay." Amanda began. "I think that I'm stupid and that everyone else thinks that I am too."

"No one thinks you are stupid, my wonderful, gorgeous girl. I can think of lots of words to describe you, Amanda, but

I promise you that stupid would not be one of them, EVER," said Mum.

"I know that, Mum. But why does my brain keep saying that I am. I must be stupid because I just worry about everything all the time and no one else does." Amanda was feeling foolish and sad.

Mum pulled Amanda towards her very tightly and said, "Let's play a quick game. Firstly, we are going to send each worry up onto a worry cloud where it can float away. So, Amanda, start telling me some of your worries."

Amanda started telling Mum some of the many worries from her list. Together her and Mum decided which were helpful i.e. forgetting to do her homework; or useless, like Tom growing faster than her or forgetting her lines for the Queen! Together they sent many worries up onto the clouds and Amanda started to feel like her brain was lighter.

Then Mum suggested that they put nice new things in the part of her brain where the worries used to be. "I am going to say a positive word that describes you, Amanda. Then, you say one and we will go until we fall asleep. Alright? Right, I will start... caring."

Amanda thought. "Erm... kind," she muttered awkwardly. This was weird. It had been so long since she had used her mind to think different thoughts; she really didn't know whether she would be any good at this game.

"Oh, yes, you are so kind. Can you remember when you put 'I love you' notes around the house for me to find? That still makes me feel all fuzzy inside. Right next one from me ...thoughtful."

"Respectful .... Do you think I am respectful, Mum?" asked Amanda, nervous of the answer but surprised at her braveness to ask. Maybe this game was working.

"I feel very lucky to have a daughter who is so respectful and really cares about how people feel. I am so proud of you, Amanda. You are a very special girl. You are also... funny. Your dad and I still laugh at some of the things that you have done over the years."

Amanda had no idea how long they had been playing the game; it could have been ten minutes, it could have been ten hours. The brilliant thing about it was that Amanda's brain had been given a break from thinking sad things and it felt awesome. This was a feeling she liked.

Mum squeezed a whole heart full of love into Amanda by giving her a perfect Mum kiss and leaving a lovely warm feeling inside her. As Mrs Leaper left Amanda's room, she too felt pretty impressed at herself. She was not sure where that had all come from, but it sounded good to her!

Eventually, Amanda fell asleep. Not quite as quickly as she had hoped, due to the fact that she was so desperate not to let this lovely new feeling go away. Amanda could also feel that the old problem was starting again, as she began thinking about having to face the day ahead feeling worried and tired. Then, something amazing happened that Amanda had never done before. From nowhere, an inner thought popped up and suggested that she stop thinking so much and start resting her wonderful mind. And do you know what...? She did!

Chapter 6

PowerPoint

Have you ever felt so tired that you felt sick? That was how Amanda felt the next morning. Getting out of bed was a wrench; it was as if her body was covered in secret glue which stuck her to the bottom sheet and to her minty coloured striped duvet.

Getting dressed was a real effort too. And guess what Amanda did? She was so tired that she brushed her teeth while sitting on the loo!

Mum knew something was wrong as soon as she looked in her eyes.

"Well done for getting to sleep on your own, Amanda," Mum said, thinking that a little praise might perk her up. She had noticed when she checked on her as she went to bed, that Amanda was sound asleep.

"It didn't work what you said, Mum. It took me ages to get to sleep because the thoughts were still there."

"Well, you seemed to be fast asleep when I popped in on you last night! It won't happen straight away, my love. It will take time; you need to keep doing it. It will work in the end, I promise." Mum handed Amanda her cereal and kissed her on the forehead. Oh how Amanda hoped and wished this to be the case.

So far, nothing was making Amanda feel any better. Breakfast was supposed to wake you up, but not today. Amanda wondered if she could pretend to be ill, but no way would Mum go for that, so there was no point trying.

By the time she got to school, Amanda felt slightly better. Maybe it wasn't going to be too bad a day after all. Just then, Maggie sidled up beside Amanda.

"Have you done it?" Maggie asked with interest.

"Done what?" A ripple of panic started flowing through Amanda's body. Amanda never felt comfortable when she was around Maggie and her crew. On several occasions, Maggie had been mean to Amanda and virtually everyone in the whole school, come to think about it.

"The PowerPoint presentation on your favourite holiday. Don't you remember Mrs Coleman telling us at the end of the day?" Maggie had planned this very well because she knew that Amanda had taken a note to the office just five minutes before home time, so would have missed any messages.

"Oh no, I never knew. What am I going to do? Oh, I always do my homework. I feel sick, this is a nightmare." Amanda was still rambling in distress as Maggie sloped off trying to hold back her chuckles of glee.

All day Amanda sat nervously dreading the moment Mrs Coleman asked everyone to start their presentations. She hardly heard any of the things she was supposed to be learning, because her thoughts were so distracted by her huge worry.

Maggie hardly learnt anything either. She was relishing every uncomfortable squirm that Amanda made. Oh, this was really pleasurable for Maggie to watch.

As 3.30pm approached, Amanda was flooded with a series of emotions that left her not quite knowing how she felt.

Firstly she felt annoyed. Why hadn't it happened? She had worried all day for nothing. This may even mean she was going to have to worry tomorrow, but that would never happen because she would work all night if she had to, and produce the best PowerPoint anyone had ever seen.

Secondly, Amanda felt exhausted. Worrying all day was tiring work, especially after a rough night's sleep and Amanda felt truly bushed.

Thirdly she felt relief. Phew, she hadn't been caught out.

Just as she had put her coat on and was ready to leave school, Mrs Coleman shouted her back into the classroom for a quick word. The fear hit Amanda like a thunderbolt. Surely, not as the feelings of relief had just kicked in. Was she going to be asked for the PowerPoint presentation after all?

"Are you alright?" asked Mrs Coleman, in a kind and gentle tone that made Amanda feel slightly better. "You have been on my mind a lot today. You have looked distracted. Is anything the matter?"

Mrs Coleman had been alerted that things were going downhill after last week's assessment week. Amanda had fallen way short of the teacher's expected targets, and Mrs Coleman was surprised to see Amanda's name had been added to her list for additional support.

Amanda had been only too aware of the assessment week. She had, as you can imagine, spent the whole time worrying that she would never remember to use speech marks in her writing piece or her times tables for the mental arithmetic. In the end, it wasn't her brain that didn't do so well on the test, it was her worrying. For it was those thoughts that had hijacked her thinking and inflated the lack of belief she had in herself.

Amanda would have probably let it all out at this point. She would have told Mrs Coleman that she hadn't done the PowerPoint presentation. Told her how very, very, sorry she was and then promise to have it done for tomorrow. However, a loud crashing sound came from the cloakroom, followed by a scream.

Mrs Coleman ran to the door, with Amanda following close behind. There on the floor, with the wall mounted coat cage on top of him, was Asif. Mrs Coleman bent down and lifted the rack off of him.

"Are you okay, Asif? What happened?" Mrs Coleman helped Asif to his feet, awaiting his reply.

"Erm, oooh, erm, ahh, ermmmmm," blurted Asif. Asif had no idea what to say. He hadn't quite expected it to go like this and was never very good at knowing what was the right or wrong thing to say.

What Mrs Coleman didn't know was that this was a set up created by Maggie. She had loved every second of her 'Amanda watching' today and didn't want it to end too quickly.

"I was climbing Miss. Trying to get a ball." Asif had been climbing to get a ball that had been jammed there in the high part of the rack for months. He was then planning to throw it into the classroom, accidentally on purpose, to distract Mrs Coleman from talking to Amanda. The cage had fallen by accident and shocked Asif as much as the others. Never the less the plan had done the job.

"You are very lucky Asif that you have not really hurt yourself. You must not climb on school furniture from now on, do you understand?" stated Mrs Coleman in a firm but caring manner.

"Yes," Asif replied. He ran out of the door pleased with his success and that, for once, his mouth had not ruined anything. He shared his tale with Joanne and Andrew, who had waited to see how things had gone. They giggled with glee to be part of something so exciting.

Maggie was supposed to be there too but the others hadn't seen her; maybe she had headed home for more important things. They then headed over to Maggie's house to tell her all about it and for more mischief planning.

"I'm sorry Amanda, I've got a staff meeting now so need to go, but try not to spend so much time thinking about your worrying thoughts. When they pop into your head, think of polar bears instead. It has always worked for me as a good distraction. You're a lovely girl with lots to be grateful for, so focus your attention on that instead. See you tomorrow." With that, Mrs Coleman picked up her diary and pen from her desk and dashed to the staff room.

As Amanda left the cloakroom, Maggie happened to be there too.

"I was gutted that we didn't do the PowerPoints today; mine was great. You were lucky though, you got away with it. See you tomorrow."

Amanda walked home thinking about all that had happened that day. Could thinking about polar bears really help her reduce her worrying? Maybe spending more time thinking about the good things in her life might help too; she was definitely going to give them a try.

However, the only thing that she was thinking about right now was homework and this was creating a desperate feeling to get started on the presentation. There was no way she wanted to have another day like today.

Chapter 7

Blink 210504 -Will Worry-Less

Amanda had a well-needed snack and quickly set about creating her best holiday presentation.

Amanda had a lot of great times to think about. One thing her family did well was holidays. They didn't have enough money for world adventures like some children in Amanda's class, but every summer they packed the car from floor to roof, loaded the bikes onto the rack and set off for a camping adventure somewhere fun.

They visited France a lot, but also loved Cornwall and Dorset. The holiday that stood out in Amanda's mind was when she was 7. They had called into a great theme

park just outside Paris for a couple of days
before heading onwards to a fabulous
campsite in the Blois Valley.

Amanda knew she could make this
presentation fantastic because she'd got
a digital camera for her birthday that
year and learned how to download the
photographs onto the computer.

Although she reluctantly stopped for tea,
Amanda worked right up until bedtime.
When she began her night time routine, a
warm feeling of satisfaction filled her body
and mind. She was actually quite proud of
what she had achieved, especially as her
dad had helped her add a few wow factor
elements to it.

As Amanda's head hit the pillow, her
tired brain pushed some useless thoughts
forward just to keep her going.

"Not tonight brain, please." She began
to imagine what worry clouds would look

like and firmly placed each useless worry onto the cloud and shoved it away as hard as possible. When all her useless worries had been firmly sent away, Amanda began the self-talk. "I am okay. I am loved, I am kind, I am funny. I am loved, I am kind...."

Amanda repeated this many times and, without realising, the exhaustion of the day and the success of the project overtook her thoughts and she quickly drifted into sleep.

Will Worry-Less was there as Amanda floated into sleep but was also having his own dilemma. After the success of the day, and how well Amanda had responded to the first stage of his intervention, he intended to make himself known to her and guide her through the next stages. However, seeing Amanda lying there sleeping he knew this would have to happen another night.

Will Worry-Less decided to work with her dreamy mind instead.

Entry was through the left nostril, where a direct cavity wormed its way through to the brain channels. The dreamy mind (subconscious) is where thoughts are happening without you realising. These thoughts then get transferred to the wide awake (conscious) mind which is the part of the brain that is helping you read this book. This is the part of the brain that is aware of everything that is going on right now.

So, while Amanda was sleeping, Will Worry-Less tapped and repeated strong calming messages that implanted into her subconscious mind. Once these messages had been learned and understood, they would then move to the conscious part of her brain and that is when the changes would begin. Messages included....

1)   Believe in yourself, Amanda.
2)   Remember all the things in your life that are great. You are very loved.
3)   Do not spend as much time thinking about your worries.
4)   Worries are not always helpful. Question them.
5)   What our brain thinks is not always fact.
6)   Do not trust Maggie, not at the moment anyway.
7)   Your PowerPoint is fantastic.
8)   Polar bears can help too.

This might be a good time to tell you more about The Blinks.

Looks wise The Blinks are – diverse!

They are a mixture of things that don't really go together. Their look is strange but intriguing, and somehow it works because of everything that they stand for. It wouldn't matter what they look like really, you couldn't help but like them.

Tell me who chooses their best friend because of the colour of their eyes or the shoes they wear? If you have done this in the past, then beware! The Blinks may be heading your way with some LIFE ADVICE!

No two Blinks look the same either; they are as different as you and me. However, they could in no way be described as looking like you and me, as The Blinks are a delightful mass of snuggly fluff. This, you see, is what happened in the Universe when all the gems of kindness were collected together; Blink fluff was created! Interestingly, as time has evolved, they have developed some human features which very much help them in their duties.

As The Blinks mature, they become kinder looking and are known to change colour. The Blinks begin their life as a light sparkly ball, bright and pure. As The Blinks mature and gain experience, they can become a darker shade of rich purple.

Also, over time, new colours start becoming introduced into their fluffy down. Hints of blue are a sign that The Blinks are learning to listen. As The Blinks feel more successful, they develop flecks of yellowy gold. Wiser Blinks produce hints of orange.

Some Blinks become Leaders of a certain quality and so, as you can imagine, remain mostly one colour, whereas others can be a rainbow of everything. Nevertheless, whatever their final colour, the expression that defines their fluffy

faces are genuine smiles of warmth and kindness.

The Blinks like to make themselves look unique too and celebrate their differences. Some decide to grow their fluff into beards or big cool fluffy hairdos which are usually liked by the younger Blinks. This hair can either be left to look wild and funky or tamed into various styles.

Some Blinks like to collect multi-coloured sugar strands from the bakery and make jewellery when they are in the 'Whey Hey Stage' of a project. Some wear hats, some dress smartly and some wear clothes that could only be described as well worn! Whatever they wear it does not make any difference to who they are or to all the greatness that they do.

You may be wondering why they are called The Blinks. Well, look around you now. What can you see? Wherever you are reading this book is surrounded with things that are visible to you. All the time you are looking, you probably aren't blinking very much.

However, it's impossible to go a long time without blinking and it is this time that The Blinks make use of. Maybe, just in that millisecond of a blink, one may have been there right in front of your eyes, checking out your situation. They are rarely visible, but they are always around checking out what's happening in your life.

How do they move? I hear you cry. It would seem quite normal for them to fly or float like other magical creatures have done in the past, but that is too normal for a Blink.

They actually tiptoe through the air and find useful resting spots in order to fully observe situations throughout the day. Sometimes, that might be on your shoulder or on your nose. Have you ever had that feeling when you're convinced that something has landed on you, but when you check nothing is there? That could have been a Blink becoming your friend and about to begin something magical that could change your life forever!

When Amanda awoke in the morning, she felt different. Normally there was an element of dread that dominated her waking; because being awake meant worrying.

Today, however, Amanda felt different. A tiny bit happier; well she called it happy, but to be honest it was that long since she had felt anything but worry she had forgotten what other feelings felt like. Maybe it was about the PowerPoint. Yes, it could only be that.

Amanda got ready and started her daily routine. At breakfast, Mum noticed the difference too.

"Morning, sweetheart. You look fresh. Looks like you've slept well. How are those worry clouds? By the look of you, I bet they are quite full."

"Fine thanks, Mum. The thoughts still came, but I did send them away on the worry clouds and it was great to imagine them disappearing into the distance. I think I went to sleep saying I am okay, I am loved, I am kind like you showed me the other night. It didn't stop them straight away, but I think I went to sleep quite quickly."

As Amanda tucked into her favourite cereal, something happened. Still to this day she cannot quite believe it, but she is sure that it did happen. The big white fluffy bear on the cereal box winked at her! As she blinked and rubbed her eyes to look again, the bear was as still as still can be.

Then it was cleared away by Mum into its usual resting place. A sudden reminder of what Mrs Coleman had mentioned yesterday landed in her thoughts. Maybe that was her brain reminding her that polar bears could become part of helping her change this situation too!

Amanda wasn't sure whether everything last night had worked or not but something was definitely making her feel different and different in a good way. For the first time in a long time, Amanda felt excitement at the thought of going to school and so quickly got her things together and headed out into the day.

After visiting Amanda that night, Will Worry-Less knew he had to make one more visit for everything to go to plan the next day. This one was going to be more tricky. Blink intervention on adults always proved to be riskier!

Chapter 8

Sunlight and mirrors

Just as Amanda was answering her name in the register, Will Worry-Less was resting nearby in an empty bird's nest. Earlier, as he tiptoed through the woods, he had picked the beautiful head of a purple clover flower that he had spent a moment resting on.

Will Worry-Less realised the importance of finding pleasure in little everyday things and reminded himself daily of the things to be grateful for. He enjoyed the act of removing a petal at a time from the sweet smelling flower head. Then savouring the nectar from the tip of each petal which was, by far, one of his favourite things to appreciate.

It had been a while since he had felt so at one with a project. He loved everything about this one. There were many needs and many lessons and that made this challenge feel wholesome.

Will Worry-Less enjoyed watching his night's work unravel throughout the day. He was hoping that Mrs Coleman was going to be another one of his success stories. It was Mrs Coleman who Will Worry-Less had visited after leaving Amanda last night.

Have you ever been to the house of a teacher? If you have, then you will agree with me that they are usually full of books, homework marking and a general feeling of busyness about the place. This is of course not all teachers' houses, but Mrs Coleman's home was just like that. However, it was also very cool.

Mrs Coleman loved art. There were magnificent paintings in every room. Her

love of art and unusual things meant
her house was peppered with fascinating
images and objects that you wanted to
look at for a while.

Mrs Coleman was a brilliant teacher and
Amanda loved being in her class. Part of
Mrs Coleman's appeal, with the children
in her class, was because she had lived
a full life. Her tales of being young were
interesting and inspiring. She made going
to University and learning to become a
teacher sound like a lot of fun.

As Will Worry-Less tiptoed into Mrs
Coleman's home, he noticed that she
was on the telephone with a friend and
that they were engrossed in an amusing
chat. An idea had come to Will Worry-Less
earlier in the day and he needed to use
some Blink magic to create a note in Mrs
Coleman's handwriting.

He set about this quickly, just in case
the conversation ended quicker than

expected. After he had found a pencil and managed to write the note (which wasn't as easy as it sounds when you need to hover in the air and write from a height) he felt happy that what he had done would work. He was happy with the result. The note read...

Amanda PowerPoint Presentation

Just as the post-it had been slipped onto the following day's page of Mrs Coleman's diary, the telephone conversation finished and she was heading towards the kitchen to make a cup of tea. Will Worry-Less

minimised himself and then gently shuffled into her inner ear.

He spoke calmly to her thoughts as she pottered around. He repeated several times about Amanda and the PowerPoint presentation so that when Mrs Coleman opened her diary in the morning the note would seem familiar.

Will Worry-Less knew he still needed to visit Maggie and Asif, but this would have to wait until tomorrow, as the right results were not always the easiest or the quickest. So off to the bakery and the sugar dough feast he went.

The midnight meeting ran as usual, apart from the fact that Blink 26302 - Bea Best-You-Can was convinced that she had been seen by a child earlier in the day and was very much distressed by such a careless act. The incident in question had happened in a house that she had been watching closely, as she was tiptoeing from the shelves to the kitchen in order to examine the situation further.

Bea Best-You-Can had not been aware of the large crack in the curtains or the daylight about to flood into the young child's living room. Suddenly Bea Best-You-Can was in one of the most dangerous, always to be avoided, Blink situation ever.

She had foolishly found herself caught between a mirror reflection and the rays of the sun which at that moment all happened to be shining in the same direction. This is the only time a Blink can be caught out or automatically illuminated (other than when The Blinks choose to become visible). As you can imagine, this situation, if noticed by a vulnerable human child, could open the floodgates to some very difficult and awkward questions. As it did in this case!

Simon was off school ill. In fact, Simon was off school a lot. He was a weak, sickly child and his mum seemed to give in to the slightest of ills, which Simon realised and made the most of. He had actually been sick this time and so Mum knew it was important to keep him off school, to stop the bug spreading.

It had all happened in a split second. Bea Best-You-Can was in the house as she had been keeping a close eye on Simon and was just about to take him on as her next project.

Simon was lying on the settee with his duvet snuggled around him. He had a plastic bin at the side of him, just in case the tummy upset he was complaining about did strike again. Mum was in the kitchen preparing Simon a drink. Due to his illness Simon had drifted in and out of sleep throughout the day, but he and Mum were just about to get snuggled up and watch a film together.

Then the moment happened! Simon was staring up at the living room ceiling thinking about his tummy upset. If ten was the worst tummy pain he could ever feel, and he had definitely been a nine and a half earlier, he reckoned he was about a six now. As these thoughts danced through his mind, his eyes were cast upon a small, squat fluffy creature moving across the upper part of the living room wall.

The creature was about 2cm high and about the same width. He couldn't tell exactly what it was as it was quite far away, but it was definitely not a spider as it appeared to be wearing some items of clothing. He never saw the face.

As Simon yelled out to his mum, Bea Best-You-Can froze, realising exactly what had just happened. She nervously glimpsed sideways, hardly daring to accept the reality of it. She could not hide from the fact that Simon was sitting up in the most upright startled position a human being could be in and was watching her every move.

A quick check of the situation and the frantic sound of footsteps leaving the kitchen meant that Bea Best-You-Can needed to move pretty quickly. Once she was past the mirror, she could reduce herself and perch on the top of the curtain pole, knowing she would be safe.

"Mum, Mum I have just seen this thing up near the ceiling. It was a little purple fluffy creature thing and it was looking at me." Simon babbled in such a way that not only did it make him sound quite ridiculous, but also brought a flush of colour to his cheeks.

"It's alright my darling, you're not very well at the moment," said Simon's mum placing her hand on his reddened cheeks and slightly sweating forehead. "It seems you have a temperature. I think we should leave the film, tuck you up in bed and let you sleep."

If Simon had rated himself as a 9 or 10 out of 10 in the sickness scale then he too could have gone with this, but he was sure, yes definite, that what he had seen was real. But where was the fluffy purple creature now? Had he been dreaming? Was he more ill than he realised?

Simon wasn't sure of much at that moment, but what he did know was that the more he mentioned what he's seen, the sillier he felt. He decided to have a nap and see how he felt when he woke up.

Thankfully, Bea Best-You-Can felt that she'd had a lucky escape and the situation had gone okay. Still, she needed to issue some advice to Simon as he slept, just to be sure.

As Simon dozed, Bea Best-You-Can buried into his dream zone and started creating something that Simon would not forget in a hurry. It involved Sloths who were so slow that all they could catch was germs and bacteria while the cheeky little monkeys were bounding around healthily having so much fun.

In the dream, Simon had become a sloth and they all developed infections which left them covered with hideous green boils and bulging orange eyes.

The monkeys laughed and teased the boring sloths. Simon so wanted to be a monkey, having fun with all the other monkey friends. He tried to cure himself, but nothing worked because he was so slow and lazy. The boils got bigger and the eyes got more orange. Eventually, he became one huge boil which popped and was no more.

The dream had made Simon wake up suddenly; distressed at the fact he had just exploded into nothingness. He had realised, in the dream, what it felt like to be really ill and it wasn't nice. He didn't want to lie in boring bed anymore. He wanted to play out with his friends.

Simon ran downstairs and said to his mum, "I feel better. I want to go to school and I want to play out with my friends." This was so out of character for Simon that his mum took him straight to the doctors as an emergency and convinced them that he needed urgent medical attention!

Luckily for Simon, the doctor, after a thorough check up, gave Simon a clean bill of health. He explained that Simon must have possibly been suffering from a virus that had left his body exhausted. This final act of sickness had got rid of it once and for all! Bea Best-You-Can had done her work and was never mentioned or needed by Simon again.

Everyone was happy with the outcome of Bea Best-You-Can's project, but it had dominated the evening meeting and Will Worry-Less felt he still had a lot of work to do. After an abundance of sugar dough delights, he headed out into the night. Will Worry-Less knew he had just enough time before the morning to do what was needed to be done next. He couldn't put this off any longer. This visit was essential.

Chapter 9

Maggie

When Will Worry-Less arrived at Maggie's house, he was not expecting what he found. Usually, The Blinks do a lot of their work while children are sleeping, without ever being noticed at all. However, Maggie was not asleep.

Maggie rarely slept and not unlike Amanda was a bit of a worrier too, but Maggie's fear was the dark. Will Worry-Less assessed the situation. This felt like the right time for what he was about to do. Will Worry-Less made himself visible by switching on his golden glow and hovered in front of Maggie's aching eyes.

"Hello. I am Will Worry-Less. Don't be alarmed. I am here to help you. You certainly look like you could do with some help at the moment."

Maggie's eyes opened wider than eyes were supposed to open and then she blinked, looked again and then shook her head in doubt.

"Please do not be scared. I am Will Worry-Less and my only purpose in this Universe is to help children who are not

as happy as they could be. I am actually
working with another child at the moment
but you are part of the problem Maggie
and so you are also part of the solution."

"I know I am only dreaming, but this
feels so real," Maggie blurted in disbelief.
She had seen on TV and films that people
pinched themselves to see if they were
awake or not. Maggie took hold of a piece
of skin on her right arm and gave it a huge
squeeze.

"Owww! That hurt. I know I am
still asleep because there's a strange
looking creature standing in front of me
and talking. What is going on here?"
demanded Maggie.

Now considering that Maggie had always
been scared of the dark, somehow Will
Worry-Less did not make her feel any fear
at all. Maggie actually felt a feeling of
contentment that she hadn't felt at night
for a very long time. She was not alone.

"Why are you so scared of the dark, Maggie?" whispered Will Worry-Less. His tone was so kind and gentle that it almost made Maggie weep. Maggie couldn't remember the last time anyone had been so kind to her.

"It all began a long time ago when I was about 5. I was in bed and had been asleep after my usual bedtime story. Going to sleep used to be fine up until that point. Anyway, I woke up to hear my mum and dad having a huge argument about me because I was not enjoying school. My mum had always wanted me to go to the school near my Grandma, but my dad had said that a nearer school would be much better for playing with the friends that I made at school," Maggie went on to explain.

"What they didn't realise was that it was nothing to do with the school. The teachers were nice, the playground was

okay and I had some lovely friends. But
some of my class were not very kind to
me. I had never met mean people before,
so they made me scared. I then started
to feel scared of everything. When I woke
up that night, I was scared that a monster
was in my wardrobe. I shouted out,
but no one heard me because they were
quarrelling, and so no one came. I lay
there too scared to get up all night."

"Did the monster get you, Maggie?"
asked Will Worry-Less.

"Noooooo," Maggie replied, confused.

"Why not?" questioned the Blink.

"I don't know." Maggie knew the answer,
but for the first time felt silly about her
fear and almost a little embarrassed to
even say it out loud.

"Maggie, I am old, very old. I have been
created from all the love and kindness

that this world has ever possessed. I have met some unkind people on my travels, but I have never ever seen a monster. You are lying here, terrified to shut your eyes, because you are convinced there's a monster in your wardrobe. Is there a monster in your wardrobe?"

"Please don't open it. He's only ever in there at night. I always check in the morning and he has gone. Please don't open it," whimpered Maggie.

"I know you haven't known me for very long, Maggie, but I am here to help you. I can't help you if you don't trust me. Earlier, you said there were some unkind children in your class when you were in Reception. Can you remember what happened?"

"Yes. I can remember Asif, Andrew, Joanne and Toyla were saying really unkind things to me and taking things from me without asking. It happened for months and it made me sadder and sadder."

"I can remember Amanda Leaper from my class telling the teacher because she could see it was making me unhappy." Running through her lower tummy, Maggie felt a huge twang of guilt about how unkind she had recently been to Amanda.

"It was I who nudged Amanda to tell the teacher. I had been watching you and I was trying to make things better for you." Will Worry-Less moved closer towards Maggie.

"The problem was, Maggie, that you didn't like the help at that time. You felt cross at Amanda because she had tried to protect you and that had made you feel weak. You didn't want to feel weak because you had monsters to fight and you needed to protect yourself. Instead of letting people care for you, you tried to become tough. So you ended up palling up with the Meanies because they made you feel strong."

Maggie was gobsmacked. She remembered everything The Blink had just told her. She also remembered the horrible feelings from that time and how right Will Worry-Less was. "Can you get rid of the monster, pleeeaaasseee?" Maggie asked, holding back the tears.

"No, Maggie. Only you can do that because the monster isn't in your wardrobe, Maggie, he's in your head," said Will Worry-Less. "But, I promise to help you. This is what we need to do."

Will Worry-Less went on to share lots of different ways that Maggie could remove the monster from her thoughts. The first thing that they did together was to open the wardrobe door! Will Worry-Less knew, that part of gaining the control back from worrying, was facing the things that make you feel scared. This was to show that you were strong and that you were in charge of your worries, not your worries in charge of you!

Secondly, Will Worry-Less gave Maggie some actions to try whenever the feelings of fear came back. Distracting yourself from the negative thoughts is always the first thing to do, so get busy!

Thinking about other lovely things is also good. Having a funny word or phrase to say often helps. Maggie and Will Worry-Less spent quite a while laughing at funny things before finally settling on 'feet faces' as something that couldn't help but make them smile!

If her worries still seemed difficult, Will Worry-Less told Maggie about the importance of flooding her brain with oxygen to activate the calming part of the brain. By breathing in for 7 seconds and then breathing out slowly for 11 seconds, her brain would feel calmer and she wouldn't be so scared.

After some relaxing breathing time, Will Worry-Less saw Maggie into bed. He reassured her that it would all become better whilst ever she worked on her homework activities. With that, they shook hands and he tiptoed into the night.

As Maggie snuggled down under the covers, practising the 7/11 breathing, she was amazed at how the arrival of Will Worry-Less had helped her change some of her beliefs. For the first time in years, she felt stronger and safe.

Chapter 10

Show and Tell

Mrs Coleman greeted the class warmly as they entered the vibrant classroom. She was always in work early in order to ensure the day ran smoothly and everything was in order before her class arrived. Most mornings, before school, Mrs Coleman looked at the empty classroom and craved the energy that her wonderful Y5 class brought to the desks and chairs that sat in front of her.

So far that morning, she had managed to mark yesterday's books, tidied up the display that had been damaged when Asif had fallen backwards off the wall mounted coat rack, and sort the numerous pieces of paper that got stuffed into her diary on a daily basis.

It was then that she came across the post-it note about Amanda's PowerPoint presentation. At first she couldn't recall what it was about. On further thinking, a vague memory of this being mentioned crept into her thoughts. Amanda must have told her about it yesterday. Yes, it was all fitting together now; it was show and tell after registration, so Amanda could show it then.

Mrs Coleman felt that this was very important for Amanda to do. Especially after the chat they'd had yesterday and how concerned Mrs Coleman had become about Amanda. Yes, Mrs Coleman would use this situation to really praise Amanda. She also knew how anxious Amanda normally felt about situations like this. She would award her Pupil of the Week too, for showing so much courage.

As Amanda came into the classroom, she placed her lunch bag on the packed lunch trolley as usual. Mrs Coleman strolled towards her. "Are you happy to show us your PowerPoint presentation during the 'show and tell' this morning, Amanda?"

"Yes, that will be great. Will I be the first to show?" asked Amanda, thinking that it was strange that everyone's PowerPoints would be shown during the show and tell. Amanda was doubly surprised that she had been selected to go first.

"Would you prefer that, Amanda?" asked Mrs Coleman, not wanting to cause her any extra worry.

"Erm, yes please. I think I would," replied Amanda. "I have worked very hard on it and actually feel quite excited to show everyone what I have done."

"Well done, Amanda. I am very impressed. I'm glad that the chat we had yesterday seems to have made a difference. I look forward to hearing your presentation after the register has been taken." Mrs Coleman headed back to her desk to be greeted by a long line of children with notes, treasures and tales of excitement!

Amanda sat down next to Robbie with a warm glow about her. This was a whole new experience for Amanda. The feeling was similar to worry but somehow it felt good, almost exciting. "Morning, Robbie. I'm doing my PowerPoint for show and tell today. I hope I don't get too nervous." Robbie didn't get time to answer, as Mrs Coleman demanded the attention of the class. Nevertheless, he smiled in a way that showed Amanda he felt proud too.

"Good morning, Y5C. How are you all today?" Mrs Coleman beamed at the sea of eager faces in front of her.

"Good morning, Mrs Coleman," chorused the class.

"Right, children. Can you all get your reading books out, please while I take the register. Then we are going to do a show and tell. Amanda is going to start things off with a PowerPoint presentation. Does anyone else have anything that they would like to share with us?"

Maggie was sat at her usual desk, doing her usual thing (which wasn't listening) and suddenly perked up. Was that something about Amanda and a PowerPoint? She leant over to Andrew. "Psst Andrew, what did Mrs Coleman say just then?"

"Err, there's no point asking me," muttered Andrew, who wasn't the brightest in the class, but he was the dullest. This was why he liked to be friends with Maggie; she made him feel like somebody.

"Psst, Toyla. What did Mrs Coleman say just then?" Just as Toyla was about to speak, Mrs Coleman interrupted.

"Have you something to share with us, Maggie?" Maggie's face went crimson, as the whole class turned to see what she was up to this time. "Thank you, Maggie. We look forward to your contribution. You will go after Amanda."

Oh no, thought Maggie. What am I going to do? More importantly how had this plan to worry Amanda backfired so badly, that she was now the one who was in a worrying situation? Will Worry-Less suddenly became visible inside Maggie's opened pencil case, and winked. Startled, Maggie almost fell off her chair. Suddenly, she remembered everything from last night.

"Maggie Ward, what on earth is going on with you today? Please stay behind at break time. I think we need a little chat."

Mrs Coleman had never seen Maggie so jumpy before. Normally Mrs Coleman was concerned because Maggie never showed any emotion about anything, but that was definitely not the case today.

Double Oh no, thought Maggie. What is going on here? She checked inside her pencil case. Nothing was there, but she knew she hadn't imagined it. She knew now that her visitor from last night was part of everything that was going on at the moment. Maggie needed to think quickly, but it was hard to think when so many thoughts were flooding her mind.

Maggie was beginning to understand how she had made Amanda feel over the last few days, and it was much worse than she had imagined. Worst still, how was Maggie going to be part of a show and tell without anything to show and tell!

Will Worry-Less suddenly appeared on her knee. Maggie's reaction was to jump, but she knew better than to alert Mrs Coleman's attention again. Will Worry-Less had reflected on this situation since appearing in Maggie's pencil case.

Part of him felt, as I am sure some of you do too, that Maggie needed a dose of her own medicine and should have an experience that may teach her a lesson. The problem is, The Blinks do not really work to this rule. If in doubt, do the kindest thing. Will Worry-Less wanted Maggie to be happy too. That way, if he

was kind to her she might be kind to
others.

From his pocket, Will Worry-Less pulled
out a tiny World War 2 ration book and
held it towards Maggie. As soon as Maggie
took hold of it, it enlarged to become real
size. Maggie had seen this before.

Then, she remembered the cardboard
box of bits and bobs that had belonged to
her great grandma and great granddad.
Her mum kept it in the back of her
wardrobe. Will Worry-Less had really
saved her. This linked in perfectly with
their history topic this half term. Maggie
mouthed a very relieved thank you to
Will Worry-Less, but as she blinked he
disappeared.

Amanda was just about to start her
presentation as Maggie's thoughts came
back to the present. She would be able
to listen to Amanda now because she
knew what she was going to do. She was

thankful for the help of the Blink, who had made her feel better too.

Amanda's presentation was brilliant. She spoke so clearly and confidently about her French adventure up in the mountains. The class never took their eyes off of her or the spectacular photographs.

Maggie was riddled with guilt. She had put Amanda in this position and no one had helped her (or so she thought).

As Amanda finished the last slide, which was of a Buzzard circling a magnificent canyon, Mrs Coleman began to applaud. Soon everyone was clapping. Amanda had done it. She had faced her fear and it felt okay.

As Amanda sat down, rosy cheeked with pride, Maggie started to make her way to the front. Maggie was so nervous she could hardly talk. All of the class sat looking eagerly at her. There was no way

Maggie could match Amanda. She'd not had time to prepare and this is what was feeding her nervousness. She had the whole class's attention but did not know what to do.

In the end she held up the ration book, mumbled something about it belonging to her Great Grandparents; put it on Mrs Coleman's desk and was sat back down in her seat within 47 seconds! Mrs Coleman began the applause again. Few children joined in and Maggie recognised that she got the applause that she deserved.

At break time, Mrs Coleman and Maggie had what could only be described as a brief chat. Maggie had already had a difficult morning and Mrs Coleman did not want to punish Maggie further.

"Maggie, I can see by your face that what happened this morning has hurt you deeply, and I am not going to dwell on it any further. You were obviously very disappointed by the applause you received. Do you know why the children did not celebrate with you?" Mrs Coleman waited as Maggie lifted her eyes upwards.

"Yes, I know. My show and tell was rubbish and no one in the class likes me." Maggie had known this for a while, but it had always been her reason to be meaner to her classmates. If they didn't like her, then why should she be nice to them. So, instead she would make them suffer.

"Maggie, I remember you from the infants. It saddens me that the little girl I once knew doesn't seem to exist anymore. The reason your classmates don't like you is because you do nothing to make yourself be liked. When was the last time you were kind to anyone in this class?"

Maggie thought and thought and thought. She had not done one nice thing to anyone for a long time. "I've forgotten how to do it, Mrs Coleman. People will think I'm weird if I start to be nice. They all expect me to be mean."

Mrs Coleman held Maggie's hand. "Do you want to feel like you feel right now forever, Maggie?" Maggie shook her head. "Well, we only have to make small changes to make a big difference. Why not make today a new day and start as you mean (and not your usual unkind mean) to go on."

Today's horrible incident had caused Maggie to crumble, but she now had the chance to build herself up. Was she going to be the same old disliked Maggie or could she do what Mrs Coleman had suggested? She wouldn't know unless she tried.

Will Worry-Less was pleased with how the events of the day had gone. He was also very impressed with both Amanda and Maggie for learning valuable lessons along the way. Amanda had realised that if you don't change something, then nothing will change. While Maggie was beginning to realise that feeling unimportant had led her to do mean things in order to be noticed.

Will Worry-Less decided to leave things be for that day. Instead he carefully parted the petals of a flower head in the courtyard, laid back and planned his next visits. One of these visits was definitely going to test his Blink wisdom and, at tonight's meeting, Will Worry-Less knew that he needed to seek some advice from the wise ones.

Chapter 11

The Bread Shelf

Across the blackened, twinkling skies of Sheffoold, as midnight approached, all The Blinks left their projects and tiptoed through the air to Rosie's Bakery for the start of the nightly meeting. It was very rare for a Blink to be late to the meeting point, though it had from time to time been known.

***

Blink 310507 - Stella Successful had once had the awkwardness of arriving at the meeting at 12.17am, just as Chief Blink was sharing her valued experiences. As Stella Successful entered the bakery, she had accidently knocked the entrance bell hanging above the doorway.

The high pitched sound had caused The Blinks to freeze in shock, shrink in size and their golden glow to switch off! It took nearly eleven minutes for the room to get back to where it had been; as every Blink could only be unfrozen by being blown into the eyes.

This instant freezing response had evolved over time as a Blink's survival tool. Should they ever be caught out by the Baker, they could perhaps simply be mistaken, especially with it being dark, for bakery crumbs! Quickly Stella Successful blew gently into the eyes of The Chief Blink and her panel. As each Blink returned to normal they too began unfreezing other Blinks until at last all Blinks were back in action.

Poor Stella Successful, she had not had a good night at all. The reason she

was late that night was because she had,
earlier that evening, been sniffed up the
nostril of a huge sloppy dog. She had
never meant it to happen, but it had
occurred as she had been waiting patiently
to become visible to a very shy boy called
Harry.

Stella Successful had in fact been feeling
lucky at the time. She thought that the
timing had been just right, as Harry was
lying on his bed listening to music, while
thinking about how much he disliked his
lack of self-confidence. Stella Successful
had perched herself on the side of the
pillow when Chrissie, the slobbering
Labrador, had pootled over to fuss her
favourite friend.

Stella Successful had no chance. She
was sucked up in one huge sniff. Stella
Successful had never been in the nasal
cavity of a dog before. It was a lot bigger
than a human nose, and a lot wetter.
Yikes! This was not a pleasant experience,

and now things were beginning to get worse.

Stella Successful could sense that a sneeze was going to happen any minute. So that she wasn't catapulted across the room at lightning speed, she quickly headed upwards into the nostril system. She weaved her way out through the ear which took way longer than expected, only to realise that it was now 11.34pm! She was almost as far away from the bakery as she could be, hence her arriving so late!

***

At the bakery, the meet and greet, carried out by Chief Blink, was coming to an end. Will Worry-Less knew where he needed to go. It was such a busy night on the bread shelves that the meeting had to be split into smaller groups, so that each Blink could have their issue discussed. As the evening unfolded, Will Worry-Less waited patiently until, at last, it was his turn to talk.

"Thank you Blink 28271 - Peter Practise for sharing your problem with us," commented Blink 241142 - Dina Dynamic. "I think we have all learned many possible solutions that can be added to our toolkit and used in the future. Every problem has a solution, and it's our purpose to help each child find the best one for each case. Okay, Will Worry-Less you have waited patiently, please come and be seated on the query stool."

"Hi, everyone" began Will Worry-Less. "I am working on a problem that is proving to be very satisfying and worthwhile at the moment. So far, all those involved are working hard and helping to move the issue on much faster than expected. The difficulty that I have now is with a boy called Asif."

"He is part of the bullying crew who are being unkind to my chosen child Amanda.

The issue that I have is that he is very unhappy, as are the other members of the crew. I suppose, what I need advice on is how much do I focus on him?"

A ripple of understanding moved through The Blinks of this subgroup. This was quite a familiar situation.

Will Worry-Less went on to say, "He's a brilliant artist, you see. I would like him to be noticed for his talent, but not sure he deserves to be rewarded so greatly for all the mean things he has done recently."

Dina Dynamic stroked her chin and considered this glitch. She was the right Blink for this job. She was seen to be a very special Blink, as her number read the same forwards as backwards. This meant her kindness and wisdom were of a high quality! "Blinks, can you please discuss this difficulty in groups of 3 and we will feedback in ten minutes."

A gentle hum of chatter arose. After the ten minutes had ended, Dina Dynamic pulled everyone back together. Each trio fed back to the group what they believed was the best solution.

"This is the difficult part for you Will Worry-Less," began Dina Dynamic. "There are several possible outcomes to this problem with Asif. You need to trust your instincts and choose what you believe to be the best one. Advice is only part of the answer; it's up to all of us to choose the best piece of advice that suits us and our problem."

Will Worry-Less reflected on what had

been presented to him and discussed with the group which result he had chosen and why. A spontaneous burst of high fives arose from the groups that had put forward that particular notion. Will Worry-Less looked over towards his wise one, in the hope that he had done well.

"Well done, Will Worry-Less. You have chosen well. I feel you are progressing well, to becoming a wise one in the not too distant future." Dina Dynamic then stroked his arm to show him that she was proud of his evening's work.

"Right, Blinks. It's time to end the meeting with our special banquet. Enjoy the rest of your evening, and good luck with whatever tomorrow brings."

Will Worry-Less joined his fellow Blinks in the sugar dough feast, but was eager to head out into the night and begin what his Blink friends had helped him with and do what needed to be done next.

Chapter 12

Asif

Asif lived in a small house on the other side of the local park. He was one of the four children. Asif used to be happy when it was just him and his older brother. He had fond memories of when they would play in the garden and have quality time with Mum and Dad.

   Although Asif was very petite for his age, his cuteness and charm had always made him very loveable to anyone who met him. With huge brown eyes and a mop of black hair, Asif rated high on the adorable scale. When he was little, Asif never minded being small. He actually enjoyed it, because it meant he got lots of love and attention which he actually really liked.

However, things changed rapidly when Asif was three years old.

His parents brought home the latest additions to the family - twin girls! Asif felt like he had become invisible. Everyone cooed over the twins, bought presents for them and wanted to cuddle and kiss them. He tried to play with his older brother, but he was now being asked to help around the home more, passing nappies, baby wipes and clean vests.

Asif felt quite alone for several years and things got worse. This might have got better quicker if Asif had had the attention he needed at home to build his self-confidence but, unfortunately, the twins grew at a pace and Asif sadly did not.

By the time Asif was eight years old, his little sisters were bigger than him and they loved it. Yes, Asif had big little sisters! This was the last straw for Asif. He could take no more. He felt angry all the time and started to be naughty. He surprised himself at how good he was at it. This also got him noticed. Even if people were cross or upset with him, he did not mind because at least they knew he was there.

Will Worry-Less actually felt sorry for Asif, and after the meeting, felt that he also needed his help. It was the right thing to do.

Asif was an amazing artist, unbeknown to any of his family and friends. Sadly he didn't realise how good he was either because he didn't feel that he was any good, never mind anything he did.

However, underneath his mattress, Asif kept a sketch book of drawings that had been his escape when things had got too much over the last few years. This art book could, in fact, have been compiled by a very talented fourteen-year-old and no one would have questioned it.

Will Worry-Less gently lifted the mattress and removed the sketch pad carefully. He spent a moment flicking through the amazing sketches and knew that what he was about to do next was the right thing to do.

He had decided to speak into Asif's ear and left a message in his subconscious mind. Will Worry-Less reminded him of what a wonderful and talented artist he was. He told him that his future could be bright, but it depended on the choices he made. Will Worry-Less also told him that there was going to be an art competition held by Sheffoold City Council and that he could easily enter before the closing date at the end of the week.

Will Worry-Less then replaced the sketch pad but pushed it to the outer edge of the mattress so that it could be slightly seen or easily knocked in the morning!

Asif was never very alert in the mornings, so it would hopefully go unnoticed by him but not by his mum. Will Worry-Less then went on to remind Asif about what he was doing with Maggie.

He suggested that he put his energy into his art, as this could help him change in the eyes of those who knew him and give him pride in himself. Just one quick message in Mrs Ahmed's ear and Will Worry-Less would have set up another part of the solution.

Asif had obviously been unaware of all of the night time's events but did wake up that morning with a ray of hope, having just had the best dream ever. He had won a drawing competition which meant his work was displayed on huge billboards across the city.

He remembered Mrs Coleman mentioning something ages ago about a Sheffoold art competition, but he never really listened to anything in class. Besides, the word competition just meant 'no chance' to Asif, so why bother.

Asif suddenly became flooded with the lovely feelings that his dream had made him feel. He knew that he liked art, as he had spent many hours drawing, so maybe he could at least enter the competition and give it a go.

After all the children had been taken to school, Mrs Ahmed began her usual chores. She began by clearing away the breakfast things, she put a load of dirty laundry into the washing machine and then tidied each child's bedroom.

Things always began downstairs in the kitchen, then a quick visit into every room from the sitting room to the last bedroom. Mrs Ahmed was actually thinking about Asif as she sauntered from the freshly cleaned bathroom into his bedroom. Why did he not come for cuddles anymore?

An image popped into her head of when he was a toddler running around the garden with endless energy. He would then launch himself on her leg for a wraparound cuddle of her thighs.

A small titter escaped from her mouth, but a ripple of sadness also filled her heart. She knew she hadn't spent much quality time with Asif since the twins were born and she now felt desperate for one of his fabulous hugs.

Asif was actually the tidiest of all
her children so his room was mostly a
pleasure to enter. All that was usually
needed was a quick pull over of his duvet
and a straightening up of the curtains. As
Mrs Ahmed leant over the bed something
jabbed into her leg. It was something hard
with a sharp edge.

A sudden thud meant that whatever it
was had now hit the floor. Mrs Ahmed
gasped in wonder, as the sketch pad lay
open on the floor in front of her. A double
page spread of Asif's artwork. Mrs Ahmed
thumbed through page after page of
unbelievable drawings. She knew nothing
of this.

A tear sprung to her eye. Her boy was
so talented, he had a gift and she did not
know. She remembered the letter that
had come home from school last week,
the one about an art competition. She
ran downstairs, scrambled through the
pile of paperwork that was always on the

kitchen windowsill and there it was. The competition ended this Friday. She needed to act quickly.

Chapter 13

Who me?

The first stage of Will Worry-Less's visiting was complete, but he had saved the best until last. His next stop was at Amanda's house.

Will Worry-Less had been thinking about this for a while. Now he felt it was time to introduce himself to Amanda, but when he arrived he found her fast asleep – again! This pleased him, though; as it showed him that his help was working well. He could not wake her from her peaceful sleep, so decided to snuggle down in her pillow and keep a watchful eye on her.

Will Worry-Less also drifted off once or twice and dreamt of becoming a Wise One someday. When he awoke, he was feeling even more determined to work hard and make his own goal come true.

As Will Worry-Less watched the morning sunlight warm up all the colours of Amanda's bedroom, he noticed Amanda beginning to stir. As her bedroom faced eastwards, it meant that it was greeted by the morning sun without fail.

As she shuffled under her duvet, her brain began to activate and her eyes began to adjust to the new day. After several minutes of her eyes panning her bedroom, they fell upon Will Worry-Less, who stood at the edge of her pillow with a very friendly welcoming smile.

"Morning Amanda," whispered Will Worry-Less. "Don't be afraid. You have been my very special project for the last few weeks and I felt that it was time to introduce myself."

Amanda smiled. "Sorry, can you say that again. I'm not sure I heard what you said just then." Amanda rubbed her eyes and blinked hard partly convinced that she had just imagined the whole thing.

"No, you're not dreaming, Amanda. I am very real," whispered Will Worry-Less. "I'd noticed that you were worrying a lot and I wanted to help."

"Who, me? Wow!" Nothing about Will Worry-Less made Amanda feel scared. In fact, he seemed almost familiar, but how could he be when she had never met him before.

"I am Will Worry-Less and I am one of the millions of Blinks from around the world. Our job is to look after and help children who are not as happy as they could be. Your worrying had begun to make you unhappy, Amanda, and that made me notice you. So, without you realising, I have been working with you

and the other people in your life, to ease
the worrying cycle you had got yourself
into and hopefully make you feel happier
again."

Will Worry-Less then told Amanda about
all the things that he had done over the
last few weeks. How he had spent several
nights speaking to Amanda in her sleep,
nudged Mum to see something was wrong,
and the many visits he had made to
various people in Y5C.

"You did all that for me. Wow, I really
can't believe it. I feel so special to have had
someone like you on my side," declared
Amanda.

"You are special, Amanda. As are all
children. No child is, or need ever feel,
alone with a problem. Even if we can't
be seen, it doesn't mean that we are not
there. One of us will usually be around
trying to help someone, somehow."

"Have you noticed that you have felt slightly different over the last few weeks, Amanda?" asked Will Worry-Less.

"Yes, yes I have," enthused Amanda. "I remembered actually feeling excited yesterday and I have not felt that for a long time."

"Luckily, Amanda, you are a joy to work with. You have listened to all that I have suggested and worked hard to make the changes that will help you to not worry so much. It began with me sitting in your inner ear and reminding you of your many positive qualities" explained Will Worry-Less.

He went on to say "You had begun to tell yourself that you were stupid because you were worrying all the time. This is never good. Worse still, the longer you say it, the more you feel it. Even worse, the longer you feel it, the more you believe it! We had to break the belief that you

143

had created because it was the root of the whole problem. Hearing and saying kind things to ourselves can break down these beliefs over time."

"Wow, I have been doing that. My mum told me that I had to say to myself that I was okay, loved, kind and other good qualities when some useless worries came into my head at bedtime," said Amanda.

"I know," declared Will Worry-Less. "You are not the only person who needed some Blink help. Your mum was worrying about you too. She just didn't know what the best thing to do was, in order to help you in this situation."

"Have you been to see anyone else?" Amanda asked, curious that all this had been going on without her having any idea but pleased at the same time to know that she was so lucky.

"Oh yes. But that will all become clear in time. Amanda, it's important that you don't tell anyone about me. If you do, the Blink involvement will stop straight away whether the problem has been solved or not. Also, people might wonder what is going on if you do. I'm sure you wouldn't want either of those things to happen."

"The second part to my help," continued Will Worry-Less, "will become clear later on. Are you alright with that Amanda? You need to trust me so that we can focus on the best solution to your problem."

"I promise. I feel so lucky and so special. Thank you for helping me and caring for me. You are very kind and special too." As Amanda muttered these words, she could have sworn that she saw Will Worry-Less's chest puff up with pride!

"I must go now, Amanda. Have a good day at school. Remember if you say you are stupid you will feel stupid. If you regularly say you are okay, you will begin to feel okay." Will Worry-Less then held out his tiny hand towards Amanda's and gave a confident trust me style handshake.

"Will I see you again?" asked Amanda, hopeful that this magic moment would never end.

"Perhaps, but remember, it's not me who does the work. It's you; you make the magic happen." With that, Will Worry-Less was gone.

Amanda lay back on her bed and held in her mind what had just happened. Today was going to be a better day; she could feel it in her belly!

Chapter 14

A busy night means an eventful day!

The next day, Will Worry-Less tiptoed around, checking on how things were going after several eventful evenings.

Maggie was feeling weird. She had slept for a short time but knew that changing her thoughts about monsters was not going to happen overnight. She did, however, feel confident that the tips recommended by Will Worry-Less would definitely help.

Thanks to the Blink's help, Maggie had realised that the monster was not in her wardrobe but inside her head. She also learnt that to get him out of her head she had to stop thinking the thought.

So every time Mr Monster popped into her head, Maggie made up stories to distract her thoughts or focussed on her 7/11 breathing exercise. This had been difficult last night, but Will Worry-Less had reassured her that it would get easier. Maggie was going to use her thoughts to change her feelings.

When Maggie arrived at school, she was surprised that her desire to head over to Amanda and watch her squirm did not feel as strong today. Maggie wondered if she was coming down with some kind of illness.

Amanda looked different to Maggie, she seemed stronger. Yes, she was definitely not well. This was not how Maggie saw things and she did not like how it was making her feel. Maybe if she had told her mum, she could've had the day off school!

Asif, on the other hand, was feeling proud. Mrs Ahmed, after finding the sketch pad, had headed straight to school to share the outstanding artwork with Mr Jones, the Head Teacher. He was also overwhelmed and had given strict instructions to Mrs Sherlock, the school Secretary and hub of the school, to bring Asif to his office straight away.

This was the first time Asif had ever been summoned to Mr Jones' office, without knowing why he was in trouble! All Asif could think about was the coat rack incident from before. Oh yes, the coat rack. What if he was going to have to pay for it? What if they had told his mum?

As Asif waited outside Mr Jones' office, he began to feel nervous. He wasn't really a bad lad, but the huge list of naughty things he had done was starting to get him a reputation as one. Asif could hear Mr Jones talking and thought he must be on the telephone. The door opened with a determined swing and there in front of him stood Mr Jones, with an expression that Asif had never seen before.

Mr Jones had a lot of charm and earned a lot of respect from the staff. Even though he was short, he had a presence that made him appear huge. Some of the children said it was because it was easier to have eye contact with him; that also made the glare he gave even more intense. Others thought it was because he had an enormous laugh!

Mr Jones was a great Head Teacher. He was strict, but fair, which meant that the majority of children in the school liked him. He had once been an actor and the children thought that it made him really interesting too. Maggie and The Meanies were not his biggest fans, as you can imagine, but no one had tried harder than Mr Jones to understand them.

"Ah, Asif, how are you today?" chirped
Mr Jones.

This made Asif feel even more nervous.
Was Mr Jones pretending to be nice about
the coat rack and then bellow him out of
the room for being such a numpty and
costing him a fortune to have it refitted?
As the door swung open further, Asif saw

his mum sitting on the other side of Mr Jones' desk.

Oh no, thought Asif, this is bad, this is really bad. His mum and Mr Jones were on the same team and the opposite team to him. He had no chance! Both of them were obviously in agreement that Asif was a stupid boy who needed to grow up and stop being so naughty.

"Have a seat, Asif," instructed Mr Jones. "Your mum has brought something to our attention that we did not realise."

Asif's mind suddenly started racing with questions. How did Mrs Ahmed know about the coat rack? Mrs Coleman knew, so she must have informed Mr Jones, and then he must have contacted mum. This was now starting to cause Asif's hands to sweat and his throat to go dry. How would he live this down amongst his classmates?

Mrs Ahmed smiled at Asif and so did

Mr Jones, this being nice was the scariest thing about the whole meeting!

"Are you alright, Asif? You look quite pale," said Mr Jones.

"I didn't mean to pull the rack off the wall I was trying to get that ball you know the one Mr Jones the one that had been stuck up in the corner for ages I was just...." Asif spoke so quickly and without breath that the sentence sounded like a blur of noise.

"Whoa, there Asif," interrupted Mr Jones. "I know nothing about the coat rack though we may need to discuss that later. This is not about you being in trouble, this is about your amazing talent as an artist."

With pride, Mrs Ahmed held up the sketch book that Asif had kept squirrelled away under his mattress.

"Asif, these drawings are outstanding. Why have you never shown then to us?" asked Mrs Ahmed, desperate to know the answer.

"I never thought they were good enough. They are just sort of doodles," replied Asif, still in shock that this was all happening.

Mr Jones stood up from his chair and walked over to Asif. "You have a real talent here, Asif, and we intend to help you develop your very special gift."

"Would you like to enter one of these pictures into the art competition, Asif?" Mrs Ahmed suggested. "It's not too late, but the closing date is on Friday so we would need to get moving."

"Would that be okay, Mr Jones?" asked Asif. As he turned, he saw Mr Jones reaching up to retrieve something out of the top drawer of his filing cabinet.

Mr Jones was so impressed with Asif's paintings that he not only submitted the application form there and then, he also handed Asif a Head Teacher's award.

He promised him that he would ensure his name was added to the 'Gifted and Talented' list of pupils at Croft House Primary School.

Asif had never felt this feeling before, but he knew he liked it, he liked it a lot.

"You should be very proud of yourself, Asif," said Mr Jones.

"We are very proud of you too," echoed his Mum.

Yes, pride, that was the feeling. Asif felt proud.

Back in the classroom, Amanda was also feeling lighter. That was the only way she could describe it. She had slept better again last night, but it was more than that. It was the fact that her body did not feel weighed down with worries anymore.

After realising she had been chosen for some special Blink intervention, she felt lucky and safe. Oh, she still had the same personality which would lead her to worry and maybe she always would, but worrying seemed to be less important now.

It was like she understood it, and that made it better. She certainly wasn't giving it the attention she used to. She had learned that worrying is normal, everybody does it, and so now she did not feel so strange.

She also did not feel alone with her worries. Her mum had been brilliant and Robbie was still there, plus she now had a very special friend in Will Worry-Less, even if only for a short time.

Amanda was still really curious as to who else had been visited by Will Worry-Less during all of this. Little did she realise that the events of the days ahead would mean that she would soon find out.

Chapter 15

Ch...ch...ch...changes!

As the days went on, many of the usual day to day things happened.

- School smelt of school
- The cloakroom was a mess by 8.55am!
- Robbie was kind and a pleasure to be with at break time and lunchtime. He did seem a bit grumpier recently and she felt that she needed to ask him if he was okay. She hoped that it wasn't because she had been so distracted recently
- Toyla Woods paced around the classroom seeking any opportunity to do an act of meanness though

she did seem rather lost today

- Mrs Coleman was as fabulous as ever. Not only teaching brilliant lessons, but also having a laugh along the way

It was, however, the unusual things that happened which made the days seem different. Amanda was stronger. Even Robbie had noticed and so decided to mention it that morning at break. "Amanda, have you grown recently?"

"I hope so," joked Amanda. "I don't want to be this size forever."

"Good one," laughed Robbie. Amanda had caught him off guard with that comment and it had made him chuckle. "No, but really, you seem taller. Oh, I don't know, maybe it's me. Good to see you looking happier though. Are you still worrying about stuff as much?"

The conversation they had a few weeks ago flashed across Amanda's mind, and she felt stupid for even bringing it up back then. Suddenly Amanda's active brain jumped in and reminded her that she wasn't stupid but that she was learning. Amanda realised that she was beginning to understand something very important, and she was going to be fine.

"No, Robbie, I'm not, and it feels ace. I think I just got myself into a bit of a pickle, but luckily it has all moved on and things feel good again. Thanks for being my friend Robbie, and not telling anyone about that chat we had a while ago. To be honest, I feel a bit daft now for bringing it up," Amanda said, feeling her cheeks flush with a tinge of embarrassment.

"I worry too you know. Sometimes my thoughts make me really angry and then I feel worse. But everyone worries. I even heard Mr Mead the Y3 teacher talking to Alison Lomas' mum this morning; telling her not to worry and that it would all be fine, and they are grown-ups. So it seems pretty normal, don't you think?" reassured Robbie.

Amanda wanted to tell Robbie that he was the best friend anyone could have and she felt very lucky to have him. She decided that a beaming smile and some genuine excitement about his latest Diablo trick would probably get the same message across, and it did!

That morning, Amanda noticed the biggest difference was that Maggie appeared to have changed the most. She seemed smaller somehow. Not in size, that would be highly unusual, but just less threatening in her body language.

Maggie was not giving off her usual angry, mean vibe. She was not as menacing, and no one felt it more than Maggie herself. Sometimes she felt like she was not fully dressed somehow. It was like she had left home not wearing her shoes or something more important! This disturbed Maggie, especially today of all days.

This change in Maggie had a larger than expected effect on the whole class. Normally, just Maggie being seated at her place made the children around her feel tense. Maggie had this amazing ability to sap her peers' carefree spirit.

Robbie had once raised it with Amanda, several months ago when Maggie was off with tonsillitis. They both agreed that without Maggie in the class, the general mood lifted and people seemed happier. This was how class Y5C was beginning to feel, but Maggie was very definitely present.

Mrs Coleman met the children in her usual manner, as they entered the room, and was also startled by the significant shift in the way Maggie seemed to be.

"Good morning, Maggie. How are you today?" asked Mrs Coleman.

"Erm, alright, I think," mumbled Maggie. "It's my birthday today and I've made everyone fairy cakes. Please, can I give them out before break time?" Maggie had never done anything for her birthday before, but was always more than happy to eat everyone else's birthday contributions.

"That's very kind of you, Maggie," replied Mrs Coleman, and then bent down and whispered into Maggie's ear. "That's a lovely act, Maggie. I am proud of you for making such an effort to change things for the better. Well done."

Maggie placed the fairy cakes on Mrs Coleman's desk and sat down at her place. Joanne came straight over.

"Are we going to do the next mean thing to Amanda today?" asked Joanne, in a gleeful but dopey manner.

Andrew and Toyla zoomed in when they felt that Joanne had too much time with Maggie on her own. They did not want to miss out.

"Where is Asif? Yes, I do have a plan, and I will tell you about it at break time. Meet me by the tyres, straight after literacy." Maggie also needed to see Asif, but where was he?

Today was assembly day, so after register the whole class lined up ready to move towards the hall. Toyla always wanted to be at the back, so that she could push the line and hopefully send one or two children flying. Today Maggie went to the back and told Toyla to grow up!

As Y5C entered the hall, Asif was standing at the front with Mr Jones. Behind them, being projected onto the wall, was a huge drawing. Asif looked nervously at the large group of children growing in front of him. But he went white and even felt a bit sick when he saw Maggie.

Maggie was going to go crazy. How could Asif, second in command of the meanest crew in school, do his job if he were in the gifted and talented group? Oh no, he could imagine it now. All the names he would get from Maggie and the others. This was going to be a nightmare.

"Good morning, children," bellowed Mr Jones, in the hope it would quieten the chatter that had developed about the magnificent artwork in front of them.

"Good morning, Mr Jones. Good morning, everyone," echoed the 360 children in front of him.

Mr Jones went on to deliver an inspiring assembly about how all of them are good at different things and have, what he called, different intelligences. He mentioned Jack, in Y4M, who was a wiz with the times tables. He was mathematically intelligent. Anna Schimidzu, in Y6L, was asked to stand up. She had been a peer mentor since Y5 and had good people skills; she was socially and emotionally intelligent. He then talked about Asif and his amazing artistic intelligence.

Although the assembly was about how they were all clever, in different ways, it was more about believing in themselves. He talked about Andy Merry, the amazing tennis player who had won Wimbledon earlier that year.

"What made Andy Merry win at tennis?" asked Mr Jones.

A mass of hands went up before him.

"Skill," answered Isaac, from Y6F, when beckoned by Mr Jones to speak.

"Practise," said Lucy in Y4G.

"A good racket!" shouted Toyla.

"Great answers. Actually, all of those things will have helped, but also, Andy Merry won Wimbledon because of determination and self-belief. Those of you who watch the tennis will know that last year Andy was beaten in the final. He could have so easily thought that he was not good enough and given up there and then. But he didn't. He worked harder because he believed he could do it. Every single person in this room is good at something. Look at Asif here; he is incredibly talented at art."

Mr Jones scrolled through several more of Asif's drawings that made the whole assembly wow in amazement. "Here at Croft House School we are going to support all of you in your different intelligences, and help you to believe in yourself too. I would like all of you to start recognising your own talents and the skills of others. Share them with your teachers."

Before the Assembly came to an end, Mr Jones handed over to the rest of the teachers for various notices. Everyone in the hall had been moved by the assembly, but for some of the children it had a real effect on what they were thinking and feeling.

Maggie wanted to be liked again and she was going to do it. What was the point of being clever at anything if you couldn't be nice? She was also going to beat those monsters out of town!

Amanda was going to take control of her decisions. She was going to use all the energy she wasted worrying about things and use it to start concentrating on being grateful for the good things she had.

Asif was going to go to College, then University and become a real artist!

Mr Jones was going to work harder at inspiring the wealth of talent that sat in front of him.

And Will Worry-Less, who was perched up on the top of the climbing apparatus, was going to use the valuable learning from this project to get closer to being a wise one.

Will Worry-Less could not have felt more honoured. He knew that he needed to observe everyone for a little while longer, in order to ensure that his two rules had been met with each child. He felt happy that Amanda had the support of her mum, Maggie had Mrs Coleman and Asif had his mum and Mr Jones as well. He just needed to know that part one was also kept.

Later that day, Amanda and Maggie found themselves next to each other by the bookshelf. Maggie began with a smile. Amanda followed with a polite hi! Both girls suddenly felt something very peculiar, a kind of connection. As their eyes met, both girls saw something in each other's that they had never seen before. A flicker of magic!

Although they never mentioned it from that day onwards (both girls knew the rules, so Will Worry-Less was delighted). Both Amanda and Maggie shared a very special Blink secret. This amazingly wiped out all the meanness of the past and Maggie and Amanda began to get along with each other; they even became friends.

Amanda knew that Maggie could never and would never replace Robbie, but no one could have too many friends. Both she and Robbie were much happier now and open to new playtime adventures.

Chapter 16

All good things must come to an end!

After several weeks of observation, Will Worry-Less felt that he could move on to new challenges. He had needed to revisit both Amanda and Maggie throughout the period of observation, but both issues were resolved well, due to the amount of effort that both girls put in.

Of course there had been a few blips along the way; the road to new habits is always a bit rocky. Amanda still worried and some days she worried about the fact that she was worrying again; fearful of it all going wrong. But she now had a toolkit of things to try.

She recognised that worrying a bit is okay and natural and that distracting her thoughts eventually got things back on track. Will Worry-Less had checked in a couple of times during Amanda's sleep, just to remind her of these, and polish her tool kit of new things to try.

Maggie's monster went eventually, and she was delighted to see the back of him. Though, she did notice that sometimes she felt the same feelings she had towards the monster with other things; such as standing up in assemblies or on her first sleepover. She also realised that this was the natural fear of a new situation, and challenging it as a 'useless worry' or 'helpful thought' kept it in check. Maggie had one more night time visit from Will Worry-Less to help.

He also felt he owed Amanda another live visit just before a very important day.

It happened the night before Amanda's first piano exam. Although Amanda had practised for many hours, her thoughts were slipping back to their old ways and it was affecting her performance. Will Worry-Less presented himself on top of Amanda's music book. "Hi, Amanda. I've come to tell you how impressed I am with you, and how hard you've worked in overcoming this problem."

"I'm not doing very well at the moment; I seem to have forgotten everything I was doing so well at. Look at my hands, they're shaking and I've got my Grade 1 exam tomorrow."

"What are you worrying about, Amanda? You're a good pianist and you have spent the time practising. You will do well," Will Worry-Less reassured her.

"What if I fail? What if I mess up? What if they think I'm rubbish?" blurted Amanda, feeling silly once she heard the

177

words leave her mouth.

"Amanda, I'm not going to tell you what to do. You know what to do. You are scared of what the thoughts in your head are making you feel. They are thoughts, not reality. Believe in yourself and show me what you need to do." Will Worry-Less stood in front of her with his hands on his hips in a come on I know you can do it, sort of way.

"Useless worries, yes, they are useless worries, aren't they. I know I'm quite good at the piano, and if I don't pass this time at least I'll know what to expect next time. But I will pass; I will try my hardest and show them my best." Amanda smiled a three-quarter smile.

She knew the words were right, even though she didn't feel it fully just yet. A chat with Mum would definitely help and so would the positive self-talk that she would repeat as she drifted off to sleep.

"It has been a pleasure to work with you, Amanda. I, too, have learned lots from working with you. But now I must move onto my next case of need. In the words of Chief Blink, 'You will be alright because you are the alright kind.' Never forget what you have learned and your happiness will stay strong. Also, never forget how important it is to talk to someone; that is my second rule in working with you."

"Thank you, Will Worry-Less. You are a star, and I will never forget you. I will wear my happiness as a way to always keep you with me."

With that Will Worry-Less disappeared with a warm glow in his heart.

Amanda did beat her worrying and realised that her mind was a powerful tool that she needed to filter now and again. Yes, she still had worries pop into her head from time to time, but she could now tell the difference between a useless worry and a helpful thought.

On the odd occasion that she got mixed up, and sometimes she did, she had her mum to talk to, and that instantly made things feel better. Amanda also understood the importance of positive self-talk and practised this as often as was needed.

Amanda understood that she was what she said she was. She finally believed she was alright and deserved to be happy, just like every other child in the world, and that was what she was. This process had helped Amanda sleep at night too.

No longer did she look grey and shattered at school. All the colds and coughs cleared up. Amanda returned to being fun in the playground and became well-loved for her make believe world and adventures!

Maggie became lovely again, in fact, Maggie became lovelier. The monsters went about the same time as her meanness, and Maggie sometimes wondered if they had eaten it before they left! Without fear, Maggie felt free. She also felt that she could be gentle.

No longer did she feel like she had to puff herself up to protect herself from the monsters, the monsters had gone. Maggie became friends, real friends with Asif. She was as impressed as everyone else by his art and liked the fact that she respected her best friend for his talents.

Asif had a new focus, and it was not about being noticed for the wrong reasons. He was noticed for the right reasons everywhere he went in school! Mr Jones even had a huge print of one of Asif's sketches put up in the Main Reception. Being small had never stopped Mr Jones and it was not going to stop Asif.

Asif also had a new friend in Maggie, and they both liked doing things differently. Occasionally Asif and Maggie would discuss things from the past, but the topic of conversation soon changed, as it was too painful to think about. Asif came second in the city wide art competition, which he could not believe.

To think he, Asif Ahmed, had been ranked second best artist in Sheffoold

was more than he had ever expected.
The judges had been so impressed by his
design, that his entry was to be used as
the artwork on next year's competition
flyer!

Will Worry-Less enjoyed his seven
days of fun and excitement, but also
reflected long and hard about the many
lessons that he had learned through this
journey. He gave himself time to meander
with his thoughts in beautiful places;
his favourite being the parted petals of
a closed-up flower head while digesting
the most gorgeous feast that he had just
encountered.

He also used the time to smarten himself
up with new patches for his trousers and
well-groomed fluff, as well as visiting some
very special Blinks he had met since his
creation. One Blink he visited again was
Dina Dynamic.

He wanted to thank her for her praise and tell her how it had made him want to work harder and one day share her title as a wise one. Dina Dynamic still believed in him. She even invited him to shadow her in her wise one duties, if he so wished, in order to learn what might be ahead.

Will Worry-Less did become a wise one in the end, and a very good wise one he was too. Now his wisdom and kindness is being passed down to other Blinks, so that they can continue the good work with children who are not having such a great time. Hopefully, he will never need to visit you!

The End for now...

The Blinks Reference Manual

Accompanying The Blinks novel is a Reference Manual for parents, carers, older siblings, teachers and professionals. The supportive booklet provides a greater understanding of the psychology of worrying and how it can impact on other developmental issues including self-esteem and emotions. It also provides lots of 'top tips' of what works best for children and young people whilst growing up and some activity questions that can be used as a starting point to initiate emotive dialogue or discussion.

Look out for The Blinks 2 - Anger - due for release end of 2015.

Acknowledgements

Firstly to my wonderful family: Simon my eternally patient Husband, Mum, Sister, Andy, Uncle Peter & Auntie Karin who have been 100% behind me and were the first people to read draft one and still said go for it!

Also to my Auntie Val, Uncle Ian & Mark for their support and excitement. Similarly to Jaquie, Paul, Bryan & Granny Gran, my wonderful in-laws.

Secondly to those who are my chosen family for their unconditional support: Anna, Claire, Hannah, Jo S, Jo A, Ted, Tracy & Vanessa, who will always be my best women.

To wonderful friends who I have gathered along the way and again without any asking offered to read The Blinks in its roughest form: Alyson H, Tony M, Jaqui S, your honesty was much valued and meant so much. Likewise to Claire J, Christine F, Sarah O, Viktoriya S, Janet S, Jane J, Stephen C, Joseph PJ, Laura J, thank you for being in my life.

Thirdly to Rachel the amazing illustrator who worked relentlessly to be part of this book, Rachel you are amazing and a pleasure to work with.

Also to the amazing children from Dobcroft Junior School who became my Blink Forum Group, Francesca G, Phoebe M, Sophie H, Matiin D, Jasmin H, Polly, Benjamin M, Jasmin S, Ben H, kids you were awesome. Not forgetting Faye Ramsay-Smith my branding coach and who introduced me to Gail Powell my inspirational publisher.

Lastly to all those who we have loved and lost along the way and who have created some very special Blinks from now and ever more and include my Grandma, Granddad, John, Anum, Shabina, Gabi and Pete - keep up the good work.

About The Author

Andrea Chatten - MSc, MBPsS,
PGCL&M, BEd(Hons), Dip.CBT

 Andrea Chatten has
been a specialised
teacher for over 25
years; working with
children from ages
5-16 with emotional
and behavioural
difficulties. She
is currently working as 'Lead Children's
Emotional & Behavioural Psychologist' at
Unravel CEBPC with schools and families
in Sheffield.

Developing positive, trusting
relationships has always been at the
heart of her practice with children and
young people in order to nudge them
into improved psychological well-being.

Over the years, Andrea has developed and applied many positive developmental psychology approaches.

This insight is incorporated into her stories in order to help children, young people and their families to gain more of an understanding and potential strategies to try, in order to deal with an array of behavioural issues that children and young people could experience.

Andrea created 'The Blinks' so that parents could also benefit from reading the books with their children; especially if they identify with the children in the stories, and their family circumstances. Both parent and child could learn how to manage early forms of psychological distress as a natural part of growing up rather than it become problematic when not addressed in its early stages.

The Blinks is a series of books that discreetly apply lots of psychological theory throughout the story including Cognitive Behavioural Therapy, Developmental and Positive Psychology approaches.

This first book in the series tackles the issue of worry and how to prevent this everyday cognition from becoming more serious anxiety in the future.

www.unravelcebpc.co.uk

Facebook - /Theblinksbooks

Twitter - @BlinksThe